P9-DDV-160

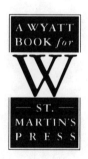

A WYATT BOOK for

ST.
MARTIN'S
PRESS

I Would Have Loved Him
if
I Had Not Killed Him

by Edgard Telles Ribeiro

———

Translated from the Portuguese by Margaret A. Neves

A Wyatt Book for St. Martin's Press

<small>New York</small>

I WOULD HAVE LOVED HIM IF I HAD NOT KILLED HIM. Copyright ©
1990 by Edgard Telles Ribeiro. Translation copyright © 1994 by
Margaret A. Neves. All rights reserved. Printed in the United
States of America. No part of this book may be used or repro-
duced in any manner whatsoever without written permission except in the case of brief quotations embodied in critical articles or
reviews. For information, address St. Martin's Press, 175 Fifth
Avenue, New York, N.Y. 10010.

Design by Judith A. Stagnitto

Library of Congress Cataloging-in-Publication Data

Ribeiro, Edgard Telles.
    [Criado—mudo. English]
    I would have loved him if I had not killed him / Edgard
Telles Ribeiro; translated by Margaret A. Neves.
        p. cm.
    ISBN 0-312-11002-2
    I. Title.
PQ9698.28.I1547C7513   1994
869.3—dc20   94-6052
                                                    CIP

First published in Brazil by Editora Brasiliense as *O Criado-Mudo*.

First U.S. Edition: August 1994

10 9 8 7 6 5 4 3 2 1

For my children Isabel, Adriana, and Felipe
and
Flávio Eduardo Macedo Soares

Acknowledgments

The paths that lead to the publi-
cation of a book are sometimes very mysterious. When they in-
clude publication in another country, the mystery only gets thicker,
so many are the little coincidences involved—a circumstance that
fortunately transforms the author's task of acknowledging help into
sheer pleasure. Such is my case here, for I would like to register my
indebtedness, in a somewhat chronological order, to a very special
group of people, in some cases friends, in others professionals, but
who all played, at different stages, a key role in this adventure. I am
grateful to Luiz Augusto de Araujo Castro and Ronaldo Mota Sar-
denberg for inviting me to live and work in New York, as well as
for the advice and help received during this transition; to Benita
Somerfield, who first heard of this book in Brazil and spared no
effort to put me in touch with the right people in the United States,
for spending endless hours with me reviewing the English manu-
script; to my friend and agent Thomas Colchie, with whom I
hopefully now share more than a birthday, for coaching me gently
in the art of hope and patience, while all along doing everything he
could for my book; to Margaret A. Neves, whom I haven't as yet
met (but am eager to), for translating my novel with her usual flair
and finesse, overcoming problems that lurked in my original text;

to Robert Wyatt, my editor, who has done so much for the promotion of foreign authors in this country, for including my novel in the first list of his new imprint for St. Martin's Press; and to Maria Angelica Fernandes Nazareth for believing, way back in Brazil, that this whole adventure would some day actually take place. A great part of the joy of having this book published in the United States actually stems from my involvement with all of these people. Regardless of what may happen now, and as far as I am concerned, they gave a new dimension to this whole story.

Part One

Chapter One

————

The invitation to the opening of the antique shop, forgotten in the mailbox, was addressed to the previous tenant. It was two months old and read:

THE NIGHT STAND

WHERE THE PAST HAS A FUTURE

Still searching for furniture and furnishings
that feed your fantasies?
If Art Nouveau, Art Deco, or Pre-60s paraphernalia is your thing,
come visit!

Curious, I decided to check the place, and the following Saturday I drove to that part of town. Most of the buildings in the neighborhood were still under construction. Except for a bakery and a Korean food store, there weren't many signs of life. The address led me to a gallery of boutiques, most of which seemed empty. The Night Stand was at the back, shining like a diamond in the darkness, a darkness which made me trip over a brick and nearly fall. I was saved by a woman who appeared out of nowhere. Between her breasts, a few inches from my eyes, I saw the little blue crab.

————

The crab transported me to another time. I drew back a little, looked into the tanned face—and there she was: Andrea. As we hugged, I thought with a twinge of melancholy that ten swift years had passed since our time together in Los Angeles. We were veterans of Venice Beach in the time California had just heard about Woodstock and was yet to digest Watergate and the end of the Vietnam War.

But what was Andrea doing here, so far from the sea, in the back of a semideserted gallery of shops in the Brazilian capital? She who had starred in my first medium-length film (the still unknown *Murder in the Springtime*) and was later to have a successful career as a fashion model? I felt I should investigate:

"To this day I remember the noise my car made when you shifted into reverse without stepping on the clutch!"

"Reverse?"

"Remember? You thought my car was automatic and shifted into reverse, or tried to . . . during the filming."

"Filming? What filming?"

What filming? . . . I drew back a little, crestfallen, almost hurt. But somehow I pulled myself together:

"The Night Stand! Who would have guessed! You, running an antique shop in the middle of Brasília!"

And she, moving slowly backward, leaning against a hundred-year-old wardrobe, cigarette in hand, head bowed, hair falling over her forehead, voice suddenly hoarse, eyes looking up from a new angle:

"Anybody got a match? . . ."

A feeling of intense relief overcame me. So there she was, my Lauren Bacall in the central highlands of Brazil, her sense of humor still the tiniest bit cruel. It was wonderful to see her again—and this time we really embraced.

But my insecurity had its reasons. For six years in the early seventies I had studied and tried unsuccessfully to break into filmmaking in Los Angeles, broadcasting Brazilian music on two FM

radio stations while working nights as a cook at Cyrano's. My film career, however, had practically begun and ended with that first low-budget movie, which was panned at its three and only screenings. The career had been short, but the scars would last forever.

Back then Andrea lived with Murilo, a man from São Paulo who exported bicycles to the West Coast. She had met him in Rio, trading the Ipanema beaches soon thereafter for those of California, where she had acquired an Irish setter named Jung and a yellow secondhand Honda Mini. She used to drive with no particular destination over the web of Los Angeles freeways, listening to the radio, Jung on the seat beside her with his tongue hanging out. Occasionally I would dedicate a song to her on KPFK-FM and, in exchange, she would invite me to lunch. But Murilo always managed to be present on these occasions, which was frustrating. Bike exports is one of the last subjects you want to discuss when your energies are channeled toward small valleys inhabited by little blue crabs.

Andrea suggested we go out for some coffee. She closed the Night Stand, we took my car and drove to the nearest café. The radio was playing a popular song:

"Hold my hand, and never fear,
What happened is our secret, dear. . . ."

It wasn't the San Diego Freeway, nor KPFK-FM, but the lyrics and the profile at my side confirmed that, two marriages and innumerable careers later, Andrea, splendid in her early thirties, was now living in Brasília, where she had opened her antique shop thanks to an inheritance received from a deceased aunt. Prior to that, she had spent some time on a farm in the state of Goiás. In my mind, however, she was still lying naked in my L.A. bathtub, in one of the unforgettable scenes from *Murder in the Springtime*.

"Remember Murilo, watching you in the bathtub?"

"Jesús, Murilo! . . ."

5

During the nude scenes in my bathtub Murilo had never let us alone for one minute. In fact, he had imposed extremely rigid conditions on the production, insisting Andrea wear dark-colored panties and a T-shirt up to the exact moment of the takes. Andrea, who considered herself an independent woman (in spite of basically living on an allowance) had reacted in her own way, keeping the nipples of her adorable breasts hard and erect under the T-shirt.

As we drove, I asked her about the origin of the name Night Stand, which, for me, evoked childhood memories of paternal cuff links and stiff-collars resting between ornate picture frames and genteel ashtrays. Andrea then began to tell me about her aunt Guilhermina, actually her great-aunt, who eighteen months before had left her a good-sized farm in Goiás, full of antique furniture, precious china, and other curiosities. Most importantly, Andrea had inherited a story—a tale which made me park the car on the banks of the Paranoá Lake, because there wasn't a café in Brasília fit to hold the scroll that my friend began, little by little, to unroll before my eyes.

Chapter Two

Guilhermina had been married and widowed twice. But she was, first and foremost, the widow of the Honorable Carlos Augusto Maia Macedo, to whom she was given in marriage in 1926 at the age of fourteen, in a family arrangement difficult to digest even in those days, since the Honorable Maia Macedo was sixty-six years old when he met her at the altar in a ceremony resembling a first communion more than a wedding.

The title of *Honorable* didn't do justice to the genuinely aristocratic roots of the Maia Macedo family, which went back to the First Empire, with incursions into the lesser nobilities of France and Italy. Originally there had been a certain amount of ironic amusement among his friends when Maia Macedo received from Governor Affonso Penna a vague title of commendation. After all, he was never even a mayor. But the people in the interior of the state of Rio, still nostalgic for the old days of marquises and barons, had in fact revered the title.

The Maia Macedo fortune came from coffee plantations accumulated by the family in the Paraíba Valley through the course of four generations. As the properties had shrunk somewhat with the decline in coffee prices at the turn of the century, one branch of the family had bought land in the interior of São Paulo and another had reluctantly agreed to live in the city, founding a newspaper in Rio de Janeiro. The Honorable Carlos Augusto had chosen to remain on one of his plantations near Barra Mansa. Considered an upright man all his life, he nevertheless began to drink heavily after the death of his first wife. It was said he was given to occasional scenes of violence.

So it was that, at the age of fourteen, Guilhermina was presented by her parents to this corpulent widower of more than sixty, who concealed a doll and an engagement ring behind his back. Two months after that first encounter, the same old man stood at her side before the altar and later that night, half-inebriated, blew out the oil lamp in the bedroom, tore off her only hand-embroidered nightgown, and, despite her screams of terror, raped her in the most absolute darkness.

Turned over by her own parents—whom she venerated—to a man who could easily have been her grandfather, in a transaction the importance of which had been confusedly explained to her by her mother along with some hasty advice on feminine hygiene, Guilhermina spent exactly seven years planning the death of the Honorable Maia Macedo. With infinite patience, she made total obedience to her lord and master her only reason for being, while the notion of revenge simmered with the slow intensity of one who mixes abandonment, horror, violence, and pleasure in the same cauldron. Taking the blood-soaked sheet which had stuck cold and wet to her back all through that interminable night, she fashioned a banner, and to its colors she swore eternal fidelity. She changed her dance from ring-around-the-rosy to the tango, without missing a beat.

As the years went by, she realized that her original terror had been made all the greater by the complete lack of any frame of reference for what had happened to her. She started to find her bearings when she discovered the library of a gentleman farmer, the cousin and neighbor of her husband. From it she took books on

each visit as one who seeks food. Through her reading, she gradually conquered her dizzying abysses of fear. Half a century later, she was to tell all this and much more to Andrea, a remote great-niece whom she met by chance and whom she befriended as if to share, in the end of her life, a fundamental secret.

Andrea had grown up hearing tales of this strange great-aunt, whose life was known only along very general lines, for she had maintained her estrangement from her parents and only brother unto her death. It was known, for example, that after her first marriage at a very young age, Guilhermina had been widowed early, taken back her maiden name, and spent four years on her own in Europe, before World War II; after the war, back in Brazil, she had married a Portuguese businessman and was widowed a second time thirteen years later. Though still relatively young, she had then sold all her husband's property and, in a supremely eccentric move (this was three years before Brasília was built), had bought land in the middle of Goiás, where she had established a farm.

Born in the country, now without relatives, close friends, or direct heirs, Guilhermina returned to the country, completing a cycle. She arranged to have everything transported to her farmhouse: furniture, silverware, porcelain, paintings and watercolors, rugs, and even English curtains. And there she stayed, surrounded by books and cats, living on investments at first and later selling off her land, little by little, until her property was reduced from a real farm to a comfortable ranch in the country. Once a year she would go to Rio to confer with the old lawyer who managed her business affairs. On these occasions, she also consulted her doctors and took time to visit her two husbands in the Campos and Caju cemeteries respectively.

It was on one of these trips to Rio that she met Andrea. The meeting was accidental. At an ophthalmologist's office, the receptionist called Andrea's attention to the coincidental similarity between her last name and that of the old lady with whom she shared the waiting room. They had reconstructed the family's genealogical

---

tree and promptly concluded that Guilhermina was the sister of Andrea's paternal grandfather—a brother she had adored as a child and had eliminated completely from her life when she left childhood behind.

When they met, the aunt was already starting to sell some of her furniture, without the slightest bitterness or anxiety. On the contrary, she disposed of her belongings as balloonists do sand in order to rise up into the heavens—and she used this image knowledgeably, since, back in the thirties, she had had a Danish balloonist for a lover, with whom she had spent many an afternoon floating over the outskirts of Paris. Later on, as her revelation grew deeper, she told Andrea that her ideal was to die without any material possessions left and, at the moment she expired, to light a match and burn the doll the Honorable Maia Macedo had presented to her along with the engagement ring. When Andrea laughingly observed that there was always the risk of the match going out at the last minute, the aunt chuckled softly and decided to leave her everything she had. Even before she died, Guilhermina had offered her some money to set up a small antique shop and help with the sale of her belongings. Andrea, by that time tired of her life as a fashion model and drained by the breakup of another marriage, accepted without hesitation. And the first piece of furniture to arrive in the shop, at that time still located in cramped upstairs quarters, had been a nightstand.

Darkness was falling. I invited Andrea to come to my house and eat my famous spaghetti à Cyrano's, made with a sauce of sardines in paprika and olives laced with saffron (no grated cheese, naturally). We cooked together, I the spaghetti, Guilhermina her sacred revenge. My attention shifted nervously between the spaghetti on one side, Guilhermina's determination on the other, and in the middle, the memory of Andrea's firm breasts peeping from the bathtub when I would yell "Action!"—and she would defiantly strip off her wet T-shirt and throw it into Murilo's red face.

The electricity hadn't been hooked up yet in my apartment—

I had just moved back to the capital, readmitted by the same university which had expelled me during the military regime of the late sixties. Aside from posters, records, and books scattered over the floor, my earthly belongings included a bed, a table, two chairs, and a set of sixteen magnificent cooking pans. With the aid of a tin of Portuguese sardines, a bottle of Undugarra, and a pair of candles, we nevertheless put together a dinner worthy of my days at Cyrano's, re-creating on the white walls around us the shadows of a certain wine cellar which Guilhermina had one day discovered in the basement of the Honorable Maia Macedo's plantation house.

This discovery was a revelation. It occurred at the end of her first year of marriage and coincided with her initiation into the world of literature. Macedo's cousin, who lived on the neighboring plantation, possessed quite an extensive library, and was kind enough to offer her a set of books he had bought some years earlier for a daughter, who by that time had married and moved to Rio de Janeiro. Not knowing exactly where to start, and imagining that his new "cousin" might still play with dolls or might not be especially given to reading, he thought it appropriate to begin with children's fairy tales.

Thus, through the pages of "Hansel and Gretel," Guilhermina moved from one world to another. Gradually she emerged from the grip of an unmanageable terror by participating in the fears of the fairy-tale characters; before long, she grew capable of actively managing her own fears. She modeled them with the pleasure and patience of a sculptor modeling clay. The idea that children could be locked up behind bars to be fattened and eaten by a wicked witch thus passed through the filter of her imagination, undergoing diverse transformations until it was crystallized into an obsessive image, the fruit of a revelatory dream in which the Honorable Maia Macedo figured squalid and miserable behind bars, begging for mercy.

On the morning following that decisive dream, Guilhermina, as though floating on a cushion of air, her red-and-white banner in her hands, had the curiosity to open a door hidden under the stair-way. She discovered a flight of steps that led down to a second door. Behind it, underneath the old plantation house, she came upon a storeroom and a wine cellar, closed off with iron bars and locked with a rusty chain and padlock. At the bottom of the flight of steps, Guilhermina was overwhelmed by a staggering vision: be-hind the bars of the wine cellar, furious and impotent, her enor-mous husband seemed to be crying out to her, pointing wildly at her hands. Guilhermina lowered her eyes and saw between her fingers a large, heavy iron key.

Under the impact of this vision, she slumped down onto the bottom step. Gradually she grew calm, and when she was able to raise her eyes again, the Honorable Maia Macedo seemed calmer too. Silently, he now begged her to stop this unamusing game. In his eyes was a tenderness she had never imagined possible. Her husband was a man of flesh and blood after all. But soon the flesh would wither, leaving only bone.

If things had depended exclusively on Guilhermina and her fabulous vision, my spaghetti would have burned, Andrea's breasts fallen, and her tattooed crab faded. However, honoring the disci-pline with which Guilhermina had conducted her affairs from that day forward, I too managed to control my emotions and salvage our dinner. In life, as in death, all is desire. In the name of this simple truth which time and literature teach so painfully, we hap-pily toasted Guilhermina and attacked our spaghetti.

For seven long years Guilhermina spun her web. For seven years, at the slightest hesitation or moment of weakness, she would get the Honorable drunk, blow out the oil lamp, and allow herself to be raped again to recuperate every ounce of her hatred. As An-drea became more intimate with her aunt, whom she now visited every month in Goiás, she asked her if, amid so many jumbled emotions, she had ever experienced pleasure in the arms of her husband. Guilhermina answered promptly that she had. So much so that she had made sure Maia Macedo—whose ardor, after

---

12

seventy, had begun to diminish—stayed reasonably active, at some point taking the necessary initiatives herself to achieve that exact end. But Guilhermina's desires, of life and death, had other sources, and were fueled by the books she continued to devour in a search that was to take her in zigzag fashion from the brothers Grimm to Gustave Flaubert.

A curious man, that cousin of Maia Macedo's, who opened so many windows for the young Guilhermina. His name was Flávio Eduardo and he was a widower. Guilhermina addressed him ceremoniously as Doctor Flávio, since, besides being a landowner, he had earned a degree in medicine to gratify a lifelong wish of his father's. Although six years younger than the Honorable, he was frail looking, suffered from asthma, and wore dark glasses with very thick lenses, which made him seem always about to trip over things as he walked through the house. This frailty had put Guilhermina at ease, making it possible for her to accept first the books and, later on, the magazines he received periodically from Europe, bringing current trends in the fields of art, fashion, and social customs. Dr. Flávio Eduardo, who had immersed himself in French perfumes and French dreams in his youth, when he frequented the Café de Paris and the Moulin Rouge in Rio de Janeiro, had later become a member of the select group of customers of the Garnier and Briguiet bookstore in the heart of that city. He was capable of discussing passages of Renan or Zola for hours on end with his friends, and had been part of the committee which welcomed Anatole France at the port on the renowned author's visit to Rio in 1910.

Through these books and magazines the cousin lent her, Guilhermina was to perfect the elementary French she had been taught as a child. Indeed, her family, if modest in comparison to the Maia Macedo clan, was well educated. Her father, a small property-owner in Barra Mansa, had seen that she received instruction appropriate to her station and the norms of the times.

They would play chess far into the night, the Honorable Maia Macedo and his cousin, as Guilhermina, seated on a sofa nearby, read her magazines or ran her fingers across the innumerable volumes of the cousin's library, occasionally permitting herself a brief question about this or that author, to which Dr. Flávio Eduardo would respond with a concise little lesson about the writer, his work, and his era. Guilhermina's husband didn't partake in these conversations, but neither did he interfere. Indeed, as reading was not among his regular habits, he had no conception of how, with each book removed from the shelf, another piece was being repositioned on an invisible chessboard right beside him.

Andrea naturally imagined that something more intimate must have taken place between Guilhermina and the newfound cousin. Her aunt replied that she was charmed by him, but this affinity had never been more than a backdrop to the main drama. Her commitment was, obstinately and foremost, to her hatred. As the years went by, her emphases shifted somewhat, but she never lost sight of her objective. Guilhermina was faithful to her husband, but more faithful still to her red-and-white banner.

As for Dr. Flávio Eduardo, he had lost his wife a few years earlier despite frantic efforts to save her from a sudden onset of tuberculosis. At this point in his life, he seemed more like an additional character from one of his books than a red-blooded man bent on seduction. Furthermore, he was fond of Carlos Augusto and had taken part in the matrimonial negotiations, believing to have done all parties involved a good turn.

And though he was unresponsive to Guilhermina as a woman, he relived in those small literary dialogues a sweetness he had imagined lost. That was enough for him. At any rate, Guilhermina demonstrated an affection for her husband that seemed only to increase as the years went by. Thus, in peace and harmony, to the sound of crickets chirping and locusts buzzing, between comments about the continued rise in the New York stock market or a speech made by the great orator Ruy Barbosa, the chess pieces continued to be moved on their respective boards, night after night, with tenderness and devotion.

Chapter Three

Two years had passed in the life of
Guilhermina without my being able to find a can opener so I could
offer her great-niece some peaches for dessert. Guilhermina's worries, of a different nature, kept her in a state that oscillated between
feverish exaltation and a sort of semilethargy. How could she rec-
oncile the implacable force of the vision that had overwhelmed her
at the foot of the stairs in that historic cellar with the seemingly
insuperable objective difficulties surrounding her? How, on a plantation actively engaged in the production of coffee, with buyers,
laborers, and suppliers constantly coming and going, could she
transform this vision into reality? How, to formulate the question
that she hardly dared to express clearly even to herself, could she
lock the Honorable Maia Macedo up in his wine cellar?

In addition to the iron will that moved her, Guilhermina had
a trump card to play. Time seemed to transfer to her, with implacable delicacy, the strength that it was gradually sapping from her
husband. And the weaker Maia Macedo became, the more he
seemed to love his wife, making an unnoticed transition from the
plane of desire to that of surrender.

The Honorable, however, remained above all a man of his
times. For this reason he tended to confuse his wife's charm, which

blossomed more fulsomely every day, with true love. And he congratulated himself on the relative speed with which, once the discomfort of the first weeks had passed, he had managed to conduct his young bride into the universe of pleasure, the subtleties of which, not without pride, he felt he had mastered.

Maia Macedo had received a European education which had shown him that a woman of class could, if guided by the right man, partake in and provide certain pleasures that others of his generation believed to exist only in brothels. In this respect he was decidedly influenced by an amorous relationship he had established with an Italian Baroness whose husband was a distant relative on the maternal side, and in whose castle he had stayed while traveling through Italy as a young man. The lovely Baroness, Maria Stella by name, had captured his heart for all eternity between a waltz and a quadrille. Taking advantage of the afternoons her husband spent hunting, she had enjoyed the young man without great ceremony, as one might enjoy an ice cream. But if this romantic episode swept from the mind of young Carlos Augusto any incipient prejudice about the forms or dimensions of a woman's pleasure, it also produced grave uncertainties in the future Honorable's spirit by showing him the ambiguity of the fair sex. With Maria Stella he no longer feared the dark, but forever became insecure.

Many years of solitude had followed, leading Maia Macedo down complex paths until, well over fifty, he finally married. But his first wife—fair, fat, and forty, herself a distant cousin of the Maia Macedo family—had died in their third year of marriage, drowned in a river during a family picnic at which (all those present confirmed it) she had eaten perhaps a bit too much. His first years of drinking dated from this time. Behind his back, his family had then decided to get him married again.

Guilhermina's screams of terror on the disastrous wedding night had, nevertheless, surprised and irritated the old bridegroom, evoking a provincialism incompatible with his aristocratic background, youthful memories, and later conquests. Such was the intensity of her rejection that he even attributed the episode to some sort of mental disorder. Sluggish from the two bottles of champagne he had drunk at the wedding party, half stumbling in the dark and probably fearing an attack of impotence, he had reacted to the situation with unaccustomed violence.

He had been even more surprised, therefore, with the willingness that followed this rejection almost without transition. As if by a stroke of magic, Guilhermina was transformed in a few days' time into an almost perfect blend of audacity and submissiveness, with spiraling moments of climax that bordered on perversion. And the Honorable, who even came to regret his initial impatience (always blaming it on his bride's hysterics), soon congratulated himself on the success of the amazing reversal.

If she lacked the polish and tranquil inconsequence of the Baroness of his youth, or the varied sexual experience of the many women the Honorable had known since, Guilhermina surpassed them in ardor, intensity, and in something especially mysterious, the vibrations of which Maia Macedo sensed but could not identify. (If he had been a teacher and she a student, he would have called it *concentration*.) It seemed to him, at any rate, that between those two important women, the Maria Stella of his youth and the resourceful, effervescent bride of the present, nothing had happened except forty years of failed encounters. And it pleased him to think that the cycle of love, opened at a remote time in his past, should be completed now to warm and brighten his old age.

Still, he registered notable differences between the two women. For example, after a night of abandon with his bride, he would often awaken bathed in sweat, shaken by violent nightmares. This had never occurred with the Baroness, although the illicit nature of their relationship (and under the Baron's own roof, yet!) had kept him tense and preoccupied. But the young bride, with kisses and caresses, would calm him during these nocturnal crises and restore him to profound sleep. On the mornings after these nightmares, the Honorable would try in vain to recall what he had dreamed of and, lacking any explanation, would fix his eyes on a distant point, where his pretty little wife slowly entered into focus, and attribute the nightmare to poor digestion. He thus resolved to curtail his visits to the wine cellar, where he often went for a bottle or two.

As for Guilhermina, she dissected the Honorable with a clinical eye, as though studying him under a microscope. She knew his routine as a prisoner knows that of his cellmate, from before dawn, when he would rise and drink a cup of strong coffee in the corral while the cows were milked under his supervision, to nightfall, when, returning from their visit to cousin Flávio Eduardo's home, or after a talk with his foreman, Maia Macedo would pull off his heavy boots and walk barefoot to extinguish the kerosene lamps on the upper floor and share a last biscuit with the dog.

Guilhermina liked to isolate, frame by frame, the specific moments of her husband's daily routine. She observed him as if she were mounted on a sort of imaginary tripod. He might be rearranging an old collection of lead soldiers. She never took her eye off the scene, which she registered in complete detail, soldier by soldier, tower by tower. Or she might reread through her husband's inattentive eyes an old German catalog of famous artworks, or an auction list. Later on, maybe days later, she would fix the Honorable again in another still frame, this time playing with his dogs or, after dinner, going over the figures from a supplier, steel-rimmed glasses on his nose. Still apparently immersed in her reading, she would let her gaze rest on him while she busily changed the scenery surrounding her old husband, mixing objects and characters from earlier scenes, in an unconscious and fertile exercise of liberation.

Just as an actor improvises and re-creates disconnected speeches to incorporate his character more fully, so Guilhermina would have her husband caress a pencil, eat a lead soldier, or discuss the crops with a dog. Thus she penetrated his world in a strange sideways fashion, imagining, not incorrectly, that this sleepwalker's method of knowing him would open some chink that might permit her to move ahead, feeling her way blindly toward her most secret objectives. In the sea of ever-shifting scenery and characters, the Honorable and his wine cellar were two of the three coordinates she used to chart her course. They were absolutely fixed. The third coordinate, the when and how, was still being worked out as, from time to time, she focused her gentle eyes on him.

This gentle regard, resting with devoted vigilance on the Honorable, had helped to spread far and wide the myth of a marriage that should, by anyone's guess, have gone wrong—but had instead gone right. Indeed, when the Honorable finally went to his eternal rest some years later, no small number of heartfelt tears was shed for the young widow, whose dedication inspired in everyone a degree of compassion far surpassing the grief they felt for her deceased husband, a man who although not exactly hated, had never been especially loved. Everyone agreed, on the rainy afternoon of his funeral, that the gentle eyes which had watched over the Honorable until the end of his days continued to shine brightly. And so they did. But behind her veil, Guilhermina was humming a waltz.

In the course of her sweet attentiveness, the young wife once saw the Honorable behind the stable, grappling at the half-open bodice of a peasant girl. She immediately made him understand, with one blink of her eyes and a faint smile, that she was aware of those peccadilloes of his and was actually proud of them, thus conferring an odd dignity on the episode. And she drew away laughing softly to herself, hand over her mouth.

That same night, exploring further the rich trail that destiny had miraculously laid open at her feet, she redoubled her ardors, making the exhausted Honorable, whose earlobe she bit and nuzzled ceaselessly, play new games in bed. She insisted he tell her of his old loves, of his great conquests and little mischiefs, of what he had done, with whom, how many times, and with what results. She asked the poor old man so many questions that I ended up cutting my finger on the can of peaches I had finally opened, spilling some of the syrup on Andrea.

By this time I was already beginning to ask myself if Andrea and her Night Stand had perhaps materialized here in the nation's capital expressly to drive me crazy, re-creating, against a semimacabre plot involving great-aunt versus satyr-husband, the tidal wave from that bathtub where, beneath the harsh stage lights, submerged in foamy water, a blue crab had stared fixedly at me from between two lovely breasts. But there wasn't time for digressions of this sort. Andrea had to take off the blouse, wash the syrup out, and wait stoically for it to dry.

Wrapped in my kimono and surrounded by some of my best Indian cushions, her golden legs crossed in front of me, our candles projecting ever-longer shadows on my walls, Andrea then took me back to a certain rainy evening, and to the top of the stairs leading down to the cellar below the plantation house, one step behind Guilhermina and old Maia Macedo. Two more years had gone by.

The invitation to go down to the cellar had arisen by chance, taking the young wife by surprise. The Honorable was not especially fond of after-dinner liqueurs, but as he had drunk no wine at dinner on that extremely damp night, he invited Guilhermina to take with him, on the veranda that overlooked the orchard, a thimbleful of almond-flavored liqueur of the type he had learned to appreciate during his travels in Italy. She had agreed, partly because the delicious smell of wet earth, brought by the humid wind, seemed to stimulate a desire for dense flavors. But also because, lately, her husband had begun reminiscing about his youth, especially his trip to Italy, when, as he gave her to understand, all his senses had blossomed at once, from smell to taste, from touch to sight. And Guilhermina now moved in shadow over rails that ran in the same direction.

Teresa and Joaquim, the servants in charge of the house and kitchen, had not found any bottles of liqueur in the dining room or pantry, so the Honorable suggested to his wife that they go down to the wine cellar together and look. Down they went, he in front, with a silver candelabra in his right hand, she with her red-and-white banner in her left, rain and thunder all around them. It was the first time they had gone down these steps together, and, in order to guarantee there would be a second, Guilhermina made a heroic effort to control the old nuptial fears that rose to meet her like ghosts as she gripped the banister.

When they got to the bottom step, the Honorable took a large bunch of keys from his belt and, setting the candelabra on a nightstand forgotten at the foot of the stairs, half opened the heavy iron grille of the wine cellar. Taking a bottle from a shelf, he suddenly made an amused gesture as if moved by an unexpected memory. Not noticing his wife's pallor, he winked and told her that someday he would recount to her a beautiful love story that had taken place in a similar wine cellar among barrels of Chianti, kegs of olive oil, and the colorful silks of a Baroness.

Guilhermina, still a girl, almost a murderess, had given a little hop inside the wine cellar and embraced her husband, covering his lips with small frenetic kisses and demanding that he tell her everything about those wines, oils, and other sweet pleasures. Laughing a bit, unable to disentwine himself from the young enchantress hanging on his neck, the Honorable Maia Macedo slid down with her onto some sacks of rice. His eyes on the candelabra's flickering flames, he agreed to paint in the delicate labyrinth of her ear a small fresco of his remote youth.

Chapter Four

———

Open sea. A four-masted vessel runs swiftly down the gray sky before a strong wind, her prow slicing the waters. On the bridge, thirty pure-blooded Arabian horses nervously drum their hooves against the deck. Held on short reins by their grooms, the horses brace themselves on a canvas sprinkled with sawdust so as not to slip. Having boarded the ship the night before and drowsed off just before they put to sea, the young Maia Macedo wakes to the noise of these hooves and finds himself sailing a foamy sea amid laughter, turbans, white robes, and the strong odors of manure, pitch, and salt water.

Would this ship with its horses and horsemen, which crossed the Mediterranean in the spring of 1880, have figured in the original fresco painted by Maia Macedo on that first night of reminiscence? Or was it part of another sequence? Andrea, confined to the limitations of what her aunt had told her, has no way of knowing; these images came to her already shuffled and intermingled with so many others in the course of her aunt's conversations on the farm in Goiás. As for me, I am like an archaeologist freely regrouping the first ceramic fragments from the floor of a recently excavated temple, so I reserve certain privileges of editing. Thus I place at the

———

beginning the images the Honorable Maia Macedo probably would have used when he started telling his story to the woman who, fifty years later, was to lie listening against his chest. Recounted in their cellar, late at night, the sounds and smells he described must have fused dream and adventure.

Another fragment of ceramic lies at my feet: this time a carriage drawn by six horses, under the command of two coachmen in livery, dispatched to the port to receive the traveler. Guilhermina did not supply images of Naples at the turn of the century, nor did she mention the final leg of the journey up to the village of Sardone, where the castle was situated. She also left out the dimensions and characteristics of this castle. She omitted details of the landscape with its peasants on the horizon and completely excluded Vesuvius. She said merely that the final stretch to Sardone hadn't lasted more than two hours (Carlos Augusto arrived before lunch) and that the inside of the carriage, all lined in white satin, had been impregnated with a feminine scent that was to bewitch the traveler for years to come.

A new fragment, this time an interior scene. Guilhermina, always emphasizing characters over setting, had only registered an endless staircase of huge stones that connected the upper chambers to two ample salons filled with tapestries, ancient weapons, and rugs. And she did mention the constant draft that ran through the castle from morning to night, shaking the Rinaldo di San Rufo coat of arms over the enormous fireplace, where a fire always burned.

Perhaps some of the hues of the Honorable's fresco faded in contact with the more selective eye of his wife—no doubt because Guilhermina paid closer attention to his portrayal of the Baroness. Indisposed, Maria Stella had not received her cousin the morning of his arrival, nor had she been present at luncheon. This tardiness, which had in no way inconvenienced the young visitor, still happily absorbed in discoveries of Italian grandeur, was to make his attentive listener impatient, fifty years later. However, the Baroness

finally emerged with a lady friend from one of the upper galleries and waved, smiling, to the guests who came to the foot of the staircase to greet her.

In Guilhermina's opinion, the Baroness wasn't yet thirty. At the height of her beauty, tall and slender, she wore her raven hair cascading to her shoulders, and came down the steps with the grace of one who has momentary recourse to her feet in order to spare her wings. Following the path opened by the soft perfume and the white satin of the carriage, and with the impetuosity of the Arabian horses' hooves still ringing in his ears, the young Maia Macedo experienced, in the few seconds it took this lovely vision to descend to earth, a wave of desire powerful and surprising enough to carry him, in the hours that followed, to an additional discovery, as disturbing as it was unexpected: the Baroness bit her lower lip every time she smiled at him, in a delicate prelude to what was yet to happen.

When dinner was announced, Maia Macedo floated to the chair that Maria Stella, with a delicate gesture of her white arm, indicated at her side. As his taste buds opened to experience his first sip of the wine produced on those lands, his other senses, though somewhat confused by such strong emotions, already perceived harvests of a different sort. His journey was only beginning.

Owing to the difficulties of overseas communication, some of the daguerreotypes of the Baron and Baroness's life had been absent from the album of the Brazilian branch of the family. According to these lively images, an important part of the local folklore, Baron Raffaele dedicated most of his time to hunting, and spent the rest in interminable drinking parties with young men of the region, while the Baroness Maria Stella did as she pleased. She went on frequent excursions with friends to Deauville and Marienbad or, when in Sardone, gave intimate suppers—stories of which, probably embroidered, delighted the local bourgeoisie and scandalized the church, firmly entrenched in a convent across from the castle.

It is certain that, in spite of some differences in taste and

preference, the couple led an amicable life free of tensions. In the six weeks he spent in the castle, Carlos Augusto had sensed an atmosphere of complicity and good humor, and only rarely noticed a glance or tone of voice other than harmonious. Perhaps for that reason, his jealousy had never taken flight, for there was no ground wire to anchor it in objective reality. And, also for that reason, his passion soon established itself in the realm of manageable emotions. Which is saying a good deal, if we consider on one hand the *fin de siècle* ambiance in which his adventure took place and, on the other, the fact that he was only twenty years old.

On the evening of his arrival at the castle, about thirty guests were present for dinner—some, the Baron's hunting companions, others, rural proprietors or businessmen from Salerno or Naples paying the couple a visit. Maia Macedo had taken advantage of his seat next to the Baroness to express his thanks for their hospitality. He had praised the rooms he was to inhabit and had commented on the beauty of the vineyards that stretched beneath his window as far as the eye could see. With their fruit he was now privileged to drink to the health of his hosts.

In spite of being giddy with the same perfume that had enticed him ever since that morning and with the wines that moistened his soul, he managed to respond to all the Baroness's questions with originality and descriptiveness, never dropping his eyes or talking too much. They spoke in a rather singsongy French that had run in the family for many generations and that seemed now to reaffirm, on the plane of language, the links uniting wellborn people, although circumstantially separated by continents and seas.

The Baroness's questions, which Guilhermina was to stalk attentively down the labyrinths of her husband's memory, centered on the mysterious country that had managed to attract and hold such a notable branch of the family. She showed interest in the Emperor Dom Pedro's health (she had met him in Paris, as a child, at a family celebration), and was concerned with the progress of the border conflicts, muted echoes of which had reached Sardone. She

had commented on the most recent news concerning the abolition of slavery, declaring herself rather surprised at Brazil's slowness to liberate its slaves; she traced, along the same lines, interesting parallels between this issue and the workers' strikes that lamentably continued to agitate parts of Europe, and listened intently to information about the production of coffee on the family's estates.

Carlos Augusto had also spoken with animation of his travel adventures, first between Rio de Janeiro and Lisbon, then on to Seville and Naples. He told her about the Arabian horses and their grooms, which, after gracing the festivals of some sheik's visit to Spain, were on their way back to Alexandria, with a stop in Naples and another in Piraeus. He had described how, nervous and uncomfortable in the hold of the ship, the horses had come close to kicking holes in the wooden hull at the very beginning of the journey until, at the captain's orders, they had been led up on deck and secured inside a fence improvised between two masts.

He had also told her that, as the sun went down, the smells of tar, manure, and salt water mingled with the light perfume of a hookah pipe escaping from some hold beneath his feet. He had had so many conversations about the desert and the Pyramids with the Arab men who took turns looking after the horses on deck that he had been momentarily tempted—but had fortunately overcome the impulse—to go along with those colorful figures to Egypt, and continue his journey to the ends of the earth.

As he glided over those perfumed waters, the Baroness, who knew how to travel on one plane without losing track of others, had decided that, with a few objective precautions and without great bother to either party involved, an assortment of pleasures might be extracted from that restless thigh which, with growing frequency, pressed against hers under the table. After dinner, she had improvised some folk dancing, to demonstrate to the visitor the latest steps in vogue among the country people of the region. The cousin had conducted himself well, demonstrating gracefulness of movement and the good humor of a new pupil to the applause and

happy whistles of those present. He had further demonstrated, pressing through the Baroness's silks, a stiffness of resolve equal to his beautiful hostess's rising expectations.

Thus, on the following day, instead of accompanying the Baron Raffaele on the hunt—and the Baron had the delicacy to leave him behind with a little smile and an almost imperceptible shrug of his shoulders—Maia Macedo was sweetly induced to stay with the Baroness and take a tour of the castle, the charms and curiosities of which they had gone merrily to investigate, down to the remotest dungeon. Maria Stella had guided the cousin from secret to secret, moving toward the most essential and sweet-smelling of them all, simply asking him to let things happen, as he had done thus far on his journey, not complicating what was essentially simple.

At this point in his narrative the Honorable had paused, his distant gaze resting on the candelabra against the wall, the small flames trembling amid his satisfied memories. Then Guilhermina, loosened her long hair and with slow, almost tender movements, removed her clothes and her husband's, and made love to him on the three sacks of rice. She was dealing with a mixture of poorly assimilated emotions that ranged from a sad jealousy of the past to her suddenly rekindled hatred. She wept inside, realizing clearly that these pleasures, brought back from the depths of a castle, had been pilfered from her through mere stupidity. Because of his age, his drunkenness, and the churlish indelicacy with which he had received his virgin on a silver tray, the Honorable Maia Macedo had defrauded Guilhermina of what she now supposed to be her most precious treasure. Thus he would die, not so much for what he had done, but for what he had failed to do.

Upon my Indian cushions, the slender fingers of the beautiful Andrea slowly open and her empty wine glass rolls to my feet. Her mind still occupied with the adventures of her lovely young aunt, Andrea had fallen asleep in my castle.

———

Chapter Five

Guilhermina's long hair, suddenly loosened in the wine cellar, stayed with me for a long time that night. She was barely eighteen when she experienced that moment in her history, and, I supposed, would not have been more than twenty-one when she managed to carry out her project. At twenty-two she was already a rich young widow, free to travel through Europe, drifting over Fontainebleau in a balloon, residing in Paris, visiting Istanbul and Agadir with her collection of lovers and friends. She had even been to the same castle in Sardone (where fifty years before, her husband had lived his passionate affair), invited by the Baroness Rinaldo di San Rufo, for the celebration of her ninetieth birthday.

With what body, what face, and what gestures had she crossed those spaces of her adolescence and adult life? What was she like, what image did she project? Was she pretty and timid? Ugly and seductive? Did she know how to smile secretly when she felt herself observed? Did she build portable, intransferable worlds? Did the gentleman who covered her shoulders with a mink coat as they left for the theater know how to read her concealed thoughts in the mirror?

I thought about all this as Andrea began to wake up,

sandwiched between the Indian cushions and a paternal blanket which, for lack of an alternative, I had extended over her sleeping body. There are relationships limited to a few gestures of irritating nobility that never get past this sublime threshold.

"Good grief . . . I fell asleep!"

I brought her some orange juice, with the same modest smile of that actor in the TV commercial who offers a glass of milk to a woman stretched luxuriously between the sheets, her mind still spinning with the sweet pleasures of yet another memorable night. Sitting at her side, I allowed myself to caress her face, and complimented my little crab, true-blue as ever, with a friendly glance. I asked if they had slept well and spoke of my desire to go a little deeper into her story, which I had been thinking about in the night and—who knows?—it might make a good script, to be written with her help. But I explained that although the facts were real, the protagonists of her story were still emerging in a nebulous form, half-hidden by the scenario and not flesh-and-blood people walking on firm ground.

To my surprise, Andrea remained silent. She looked at me as if seeing me for the first time. After a while she explained, hesitating a bit, that for her, it had been different. Night after night, in the course of her numerous visits to the farm in Goiás, her aunt, sitting in a rocking chair with a cat on her lap, had spun out for her each one of the scenes in absolutely minute detail. How could she not see everything? What interest would her aunt have, at that point, already tired and half sick, in making her life more colorful than it really had been?

True, she had found it difficult at first to imagine that, behind the wrinkles of the old lady, there had once been a young woman who, in the thirties in Brazil, had had the courage to execute a cold-blooded crime, preceded by long years of pretense, and had not only carried out her plan but had shown no signs of anxiety or remorse. She even once believed that her aunt, during the half century that the story hibernated in her head, had altered the facts

---

somewhat—not to embroider what had occurred but simply because of the confusion that age often brings. After all, if *Grimm's Fairy Tales* had been the basis for the whole saga, it seemed reasonable that Guilhermina, while giving shape to her story, might resort to some scenes from her original source or possibly borrow some more colorful character from the trunk of her childhood, as one salvages a favorite doll.

But Andrea had ended up believing the whole story—setting, characters, and illustrations included—when she discovered an old letter which, years after the Honorable's death, had been written to her aunt by his cousin and neighbor, Flávio Eduardo. It revealed the suspicions he had always had but never made public. In this letter, to which Guilhermina herself referred more than once (though she didn't show it to Andrea), Flávio Eduardo had not made threats nor presumed to judge her. He had simply dissected in detail what he supposed to have happened and, message delivered, had said good-bye—literally, for he died almost immediately afterward. But that letter, like an unexpected beam of light that suddenly pierces the darkness by chance, had legitimized the whole story, giving the tone of documentary to what had up to that point seemed more like fiction.

Andrea had found the letter some months after Guilhermina's funeral, when she was cleaning out an old cupboard before sending it to the Night Stand for a client. It was in a box where her aunt had apparently kept correspondence, documents, and a few souvenirs of her childhood, adolescence, and adult life. She had read that letter but postponed examining the rest of the memorabilia more carefully, partly out of respect for her aunt, partly through the shame of having doubted the truth of her story. "What if . . . ?"

An old box of letters and souvenirs?

It was Sunday, a day of blue skies and sunshine. My personal projects as a newly arrived resident of the capital could be easily put aside. While we fixed breakfast, I asked her more about the wonderful box. Andrea smiled and, turning the imaginary handle that

old-time cameramen used to roll their sixteen frames a second, proposed that we go spend a day or two on the farm, where we could bathe in a waterfall and examine the old box of souvenirs.

After a stop at her place for a shower, a change of clothes, and some birdseed for her canaries, we drove off toward Pirenópolis. The road, still empty at that hour of the morning, was a welcome sight after so many weeks of symmetry and reinforced concrete. Years before, I had photographed Pirenópolis and its Cavalry Parade for a newspaper in Rio. Of the Cavalry Parade, only a few photos were left of drunks wearing masks, stumbling through the streets with their empty bottles, and the memory of music with a strong hypnotic beat pulsing through the night over the city's outdoor loudspeakers. Something else had happened on that trip, a brief love affair I promised not to reveal.

We arrived after a two-hour drive. The farm, nestled in a small valley, was now reduced to a few dozen acres and, as one could easily see, had known better times. The whitewashed house, built between an orchard and a road that twisted down toward the waterfall, was spotted with mud, and some of the windows were coming loose from their hinges. The roof had tiles missing, the gutters were rusty, and the porch railing seemed to lean over the patio. But the inside, spacious and pleasant, still had some signs of the pride with which it had been conceived, from the pine floors to the designs carved in the window frames, the blue Portuguese tiles in the kitchen, and the old-fashioned bath fixtures.

The caretakers and their three children received us amid barking dogs and quacking ducks. Two or three pigs were rooting happily in their pen, beside a skinny horse that swatted flies with its tail. Several cages holding birds of various colors and sizes graced the branches of two almond trees in front of the house. From the highest of these branches hung a rope swing, and perched on it was a rooster which observed our arrival with severity, not suspecting that two hours later, we would exclaim in his honor, "Mmmm, how delicious!"

"Who would have guessed, that old rooster would be so tender . . ."

. . . already eyeing the ambrosia dessert waiting in the kitchen. In the wings, between the memory of an invigorating plunge in the waterfall and the perspective of a night in a hammock under the stars, Guilhermina's box awaited the three solemn taps that would announce its entrance onto the stage.

Actually, it was a hatbox, and still bore on its lid shreds of travel tags where I could guess, rather than read, Compagnie des Transports Maritimes and, on the other side, SS *Manitoba*. Inside it, carefully tied with silk ribbons in several colors, we found three small stacks of papers and letters which we put to one side, and several manila envelopes in various sizes, without any notations written on the outside. According to Andrea, who had only looked through the box once quickly, these envelopes contained a little of everything: yellowed photos from Guilhermina's years of marriage and other periods, locks of hair, a moth-eaten black mask, theater programs, old receipts for tickets, paper money from European countries, and even recipes for seventeenth-century Italian desserts.

Face to face with the hatbox at last, I now hesitated to open the envelopes. Guilhermina and her Honorable ran the risk of losing the freedom of movement they had enjoyed so far, bouncing upward and downward, like musical notes on a sheet: now ugly, now beautiful, now young, now old, now reading, now thinking, now loving, now dying. They were about to be "seen." And some profiles are better preserved when less clearly defined.

The first photo we looked at showed a little girl of three standing on a footpath with some trees in the background. Long dress reaching down to her shoes, sleeves to her wrists, rigid bows at her waist and in her hair, and a small hoop held up in her right hand, the child looked directly into the camera without smiling, her head bent downward and her eyes gazing up at an angle. On the back of the photograph, in brown ink and gothic letters, was

the inscription: *Lunch at the home of Pedro Paulo de Moraes, June 7, 1915.*

At the age of three, Guilhermina already held her small metal hoop with the determination of one who knows the value of a solid sword-hilt. Her parents, who eleven years later were to turn her over without hesitation to a man nearing the end of his life, must have been standing nearby, waving from somewhere behind the photographer and his tripod. What had they been like? On that visit to Pedro Paulo de Moraes, had her father worn a frock coat?

No, he was in shirtsleeves, smiling widely and holding his daughter on his lap, sitting on a garden bench. On the back, the same inscription as to date and locale. Guilhermina was now looking firmly at the ground and stretching her arm out to reach the small hoop that had fallen beside her father's feet. Her hand, out of focus, was full of life among the sepia tones of the garden. You could feel her tension and almost hear her cries.

Another picture: her mother. She was wearing a hat and the classic lace-trimmed blouse buttoned up to the neck. Hands crossed in her lap, she was predictable in her posture and desires. Her well-behaved features revealed a disciplined nature. But the eyes facing the camera with a trace of irony seemed to have a life of their own. And when, later that evening, we found a photo of Guilhermina at Fouquet's, standing among five happy frock-coated men with their champagne glasses raised in midair, I realized we had retrieved, in her smile, the seed of that 1915 look.

"This guy must be your grandfather."

"You're right . . . it must be he. . . . Gee, my grandfather. Hi, Grandpa!"

"Grandpa, say hello to your granddaughter Andrea."

The little boy obviously hated his sailor suit. For some reason the outfit didn't look very good on him, maybe because he was too old for it. The material squeezed his body in and offended his inclinations toward a more adult costume. He refused to be cheerful,

but held his sister's hand firmly, while she gave us a smile for the first time. It was a gap-toothed smile that left no doubt whatsoever: her big brother was wonderful! And her beautiful mother and father were marvelous, too! And life was even sweeter than the huge sticky lollipop she held up in offering to the family that called her name from behind the camera.

In the next photo the family was no longer calling out. On the contrary, seven couples now looked at me with a sober air, the women serenely seated on their well-kept secrets, the men standing behind them, holding their hats, each with his little mustache and the same condescending air. On the floor, between cousins of all ages, Guilhermina, with no lollipop and the same grin, tried to amuse the ever-serious sailor at her side.

There was work here for a team of researchers. Before going any further with the images, I gave in to the temptation to investigate the sounds a little, carefully undoing one of the small packages of letters. *Guilhermine, tes cheveux rouges me hantent . . . . Guilhermina, your red hair* (so she was a redhead, Andrea's great-aunt? a touch of color surfaced) *bewitches me, no, pursues me, drives me crazy.* The signature was that of a Paul Nat. The name was vaguely familiar and made me think of a critic who had written a book about Poulenc or George Auric. Maybe it was he: further on, the letter mentioned his *friend Claude,* with whom he had just had lunch and who had spent the afternoon discussing the works of Erik Satie. The letter transported us directly into the music world of Paris in the twenties. Would Guilhermina have known and frequented such circles?

Andrea remembered that indeed, between the Danish balloonist and a mysterious figure who owned a cabaret and specialized in dwarfs that performed a striptease act, her aunt had mentioned a pianist, but she hadn't caught the name, or her aunt hadn't revealed it. *Why didn't you come yesterday? Was the food last*

Sunday really that bad? Guilhermina, what kind of surrender was that, followed so soon by a disappearance? Are you perhaps teasing me? (Par hasard, te moquerais-tu de moi?) Come back, for the love of all the gods— including the ones in your country that you tell me so much about, that strange land of musicians, slaves, witches, and grasshoppers. . . ."

Chapter Six

The night was wearing on. Many old photos, letters, notes, cards, and first-communion announcements had paraded under our eyes. At first we were curious, then attentive, and finally surprised. Andrea now retraced in my company the path she had followed listening to her aunt talk during the weekends spent at that same farm. A faithful fellow traveler, I reconstructed by her side some of the stages of the journey, heroically resisting the temptation to give movement and life to the photos—resisting, in short, the temptation to make a film.

Some snapshots had nothing written on the back, and looked like free-floating images, full of unknown characters in unidentified places that could have been in this hatbox or any other. What were those two women doing riding elephants? And who was the man dressed in white by their side? And another man, rowing his boat in a short-sleeved shirt and straw hat? Who was the young fellow serving the wine, his back turned to us? And the woman sitting on the grass, smiling at him, hair tossed back? That baby, lifted up in the arms of a little girl sitting in a swing—whom did it belong to? Some letters were hardly more than notes, often bearing the name of a person or city but sometimes only a date—what might they conceal? In spite of the difficulties, it was seductive to put together this old puzzle, fitting words to images, small details to characters.

Actually, the material Guilhermina left us was not so abundant, considering the multitude of stages she had been through in her almost eighty years. There was very little, for example, from her childhood or adolescence, and almost nothing from her first marriage. There was no picture of the Honorable or of the plantation where the key episode of her life had taken place. Her four years in Europe, on the other hand, seemed better documented. It was obvious that at that point she had finally gathered the reins of her destiny into her hands.

Even so, those years of travel contained blank spaces of whole months, or important cities mentioned only in passing in some letter about another subject. Like Agadir, mentioned in connection with a French explorer whom she met on his return from the forbidden citadel of Smara (he died not long afterward of diphtheria), or Istanbul, where a menu (in its margins we could read *banquet offered by Edouard*) informed us that the traveler had started her dinner with *Perles de la Mer Noire sur Socle de Glace,* afterward having a *Potage de Tortue claire* and, to accompany the main dish (vapor-cooked duck seasoned with herbs) *Tomates Clamart.*

How had those tomatoes been prepared? Seasoned with garlic, to contrast with the delicacy of the steamed duck? How did the wines taste—a Chablis Bougros 1917 and a Charmes Chambertin 1921? Might someone have exclaimed, as did Baudelaire, that *the soul of the wines sang in the bottles?* What did it matter, the setting was Istanbul, the year 1937, and probably there had existed a terrace over the Bosporus with moonlight on the minarets. (Or had it rained torrentially?) And who was this Edouard, with whom the young widow had shared such a magnificent dinner? An honorary consul carrying out a social obligation as a favor to a third party? Or the owner of El Bolero, to whom Guilhermina referred cryptically when she mentioned a small moment of weakness to her niece?

"The four dwarfs were quite green," Guilhermina had said with a melancholy sigh, speaking of that person from the Parisian *bas-fond* to whom she had yielded in a moment of caprice, in a train between Geneva and Milan. And the dwarfs were green because they went on stage totally covered in leaves, which they took off one by one to the rhythmic clapping of an audience in long gowns and tailcoats, as flutes were played by two satyrs hopping about in the shadows. But Guilhermina had changed the subject quickly, leaving the four female dwarfs and their leaves up in the air. And though we shuffled through the hatbox in search of clues, we found nothing about that odd relationship, which had begun in a wagon-restaurant near the Simplon Pass, only to derail at some point in the itinerary and give way to other people, other cadences.

But about Paul Nat, the pianist, we learned more. Guilhermina's relationship with him had begun with cadences from Mozart. Their meeting was documented in a letter in which he himself described, with the sentimental detail of an adolescent, a small sentence scribbled three years before in the margins of a program from the Salle Gaveau, where he had called Guilhermina's attention to the second movement of a Mozart concerto which contained *a cadence almost as lovely as your profile of fire and dreams.* The beautiful message had come folded up inside a little box of bonbons. How far apart had they been sitting? He a little behind her, on the diagonal, his eyes fixed on the lovely profile of the young woman unknown to him? Had she been accompanied by a lady friend? Had she smiled at the stranger's brashness? Or had she remained serious, not even turning in the direction the usher indicated with a yawn? Had she eaten the bonbons? During the interval of the concert he had offered her a glass of champagne which, according to the letter, she had accepted. Nevertheless, *three cruel and atrociously interminable years* had transpired before, *on that first vibrant afternoon of summer,* he had finally encountered her again in Montparnasse, standing in front of a Joan Miró sketch, two steps away from the door of the building where he lived. *An extraordinary coincidence*—and to me it was even more extraordinary to imagine Miró sketches in the window of a little gallery that might also have had Braque or Matisse canvases on its walls.

—

38

They had gone up to his studio, *tout juste pour prendre un petit café,* she hesitating, he insisting, and, once they got there (it was hot, after all), they had decided on a chilled Muscadet instead. In homage to their re-encounter, he had improvised the famous Mozart cadence for her on his piano, while she stood looking at the somber-hued wallpaper with its scenes from Watteau. Later, maybe about the time of *Trois pièces en forme de poire,* she came and sat beside him on the piano bench, watching his left hand slide over the keyboard while his right suddenly touched her warm knee. In the next paragraph, the lovers reappeared asleep in the bedroom, *the yellow light on your white skin, the small vase of poppies between the books on the shelf, your red hair against the white sheets like a Renoir.*

Like a Renoir . . . soon after this, an alcove by the sea provided the backdrop for another summer image. The ocean was sunlit. The couple in the photo wore bathing costumes and carried towels over their shoulders. Hair blown back, they embraced tenderly at the water's edge and smiled radiantly at *Monsieur Jean Lambert, Photographe,* who had autographed his work in meticulous white letters at the bottom. In the background, barely visible on the ocean, was a tiny hydroplane.

The first image of the adult Guilhermina, mistress of herself and her destiny, showed her smiling with the same enchantment she had once felt for a certain young sailor who had disappeared in the shipwreck of her childhood. Her eyes were wide with pleasure; there was the same intensity of joy. But between these two snapshots, an old man had died of starvation behind bars in a dark cellar. Hence the difference between her smile, full of life, and that of Paul Nat, almost naive.

Nice, in the bright sunlight of 1938, was living its last summer before the war. On the back of the photo, Paul Nat had borrowed a quote from Banville to express his profound endearment and delight: *"Nice, like you, a goddess laughing and vibrant, emerging from a jet of foam beneath the kiss of the sun . . ."*

Guilhermina did indeed seem to have emerged from a jet of

sea spray. Even before looking at the photo I could see her beauty reflected in Andrea's wondering expression. There was something besides the clear eyes and red curls, the air of a laughing and vibrant goddess—something the lover saw, but could not preserve. There was, above all, a tranquility that emanated from a woman who had won the right to enjoy every pleasure life could offer, an aura that drew our eyes to her.

And not only our eyes. Others had also been fascinated, as soon became evident in snapshots of a walk through the Bois de Boulogne and a late-afternoon tea party in the Pré Catelan. In the Bois, three young ladies held their hats laughingly as the wind blew. The most striking thing about that fleeting moment was the way one of them looked at Guilhermina, on whom all the afternoon light was concentrated. At the Pré Catalan, almost immediately afterward (or had it been before?) the same woman had an arm around our goddess, whose head, tenderly leaning backward, suggested grace and abandon.

Then the unexpected occurred. Between these women, captured by surprise at a precise moment in their lives, and ourselves, their intrusive observers half a century later, two sheets of yellowed paper suddenly fell, unstuck from the cardboard that molded the photos, and lay softly on the tablecloth in front of us.

The yellowed pieces of paper bore screams, not words. After the serene photo of the walk in the park, they took us by surprise. We reread the short texts, shocked at their unexpected indignation. Was the young widow, still wrapped in her splendorous mantle of vibrant goddess, about to reveal clay feet? Andrea turned pale at my side.

The first of the notes that fell out from behind the snapshot was like a bomb exploding. *Ce soir je t'ai mille fois fouetté en mon imagination, sale petite garce!* (Tonight I've whipped you a thousand times in my imagination, you filthy little bitch!) Guilhermina, maybe years later, had stapled the astonishing message to a newspaper clipping, dated October 23, 1937, and containing a short text with a grainy photograph of the same beautiful young woman who, on another day and in another picture, had tenderly put an arm around her. Her name was Marie-France Jocelin. She had merited this attention from the press because an establishment belonging to her had been closed by the police. The accusation: exploitation of minors.

The text said that, among other perversions, some clients, undressed and tied to small vertical posts put up in front of the audience, had been whipped by half-naked children. The proprietress conceded that the visas of some of the artists she had brought from Italy were indeed irregular, but alleged in her own defense that she had been deceived by these artists as to their age. Concerning the matter of whipping, she insisted that her clients were very well aware of what they were doing. And she added that the *préfet de police* himself had dined in her cabaret more than once and made no complaints about the food or the show. Two lines further down, the *préfet* vehemently denied he had ever been there.

The photo that illustrated the disagreeable *fait divers* had been taken at a more festive moment, probably on some opening night. In it, Marie-France smiled widely as she took her bows before an invisible audience, in a jovial, informal pose, body bent slightly forward, four naked little girls just behind her, waving to the public. *Four naked little girls?* Although the image was fuzzy, we saw at once they weren't little girls, but dwarfs: *the four green dwarfs*. The clipping confirmed it: the name of the establishment was El Bolero. Then what about that encounter on the train?

During that trip from Geneva to Milan, two women, moved by a mutual empathy, had embraced in the Simplon tunnel. And, the train, coming out into the open, had taken the only direction possible on journeys of that kind, the direction of an emotional roller coaster. As proof we had these newly discovered notes: no hatred or humiliation that intense could have resulted from half affection or half surrender. No, that night on the train had been replete: a night of champagne, bells, shadows, lights, sudden curves beneath the sheets—and lots of smoke.

But the destruction was as evident as the passion. And something very destructive had certainly happened, who knows, maybe weeks, months, or years later. For the wounded lover tried in her cold, cutting letter to lash Guilhermina with her frustration and jealousy, screaming to the heavens, *"Ce soir . . ."*

The bitterness of the words, the allusion to physical violence, the fierce intimacy of that *sale petite garce* all contrasted with the purity on the faces of those women and the delicacy of the gestures captured by the photos we still held. For us, concerned with Guilhermina and the course of her life, these discoveries constituted a surprising landmark on the long road that twisted between Barra Mansa and Pirenópolis, with stops in Paris and Agadir. (Curiously, in a counterpoint image, the back of the clipping showed half of Greta Garbo's face, with the news of her arrival in Paris for the opening of *Camille*).

On the table, the other note was still waiting. Its sentences, like electric currents suddenly inverted, seemed to want to alter the poles of suffering and humiliation. Marie-France, desperate before, now condemned Guilhermina peremptorily to the most absolute ostracism: *"It's no good begging, you had your chance, you won't get another. Kill yourself if you want, that won't stop me from going back on the stage (celà ne m'empêchera pas de remonter sur scène) or give in to these men that follow you like animals in heat. I leave today for Sologne, then on to Agadir. Go back to your country! I wish you had never left it in the first place. Or go to hell. But leave me alone. M."*

End of the line, end of the relationship, cars derailed. End of the record of a story that was summed up in two notes and three photos, with half a Greta Garbo thrown in.

So that was why Guilhermina had gone to Agadir: to try in

vain to find Marie-France, with her whips, green dwarfs, firm half-open thighs, and unexpected pleasures. But in Agadir she had found nothing, as the hatbox sadly confirmed, except a French explorer obsessed by a mysterious citadel. (Had she flown to Morocco in the hydroplane that rested on other waters in her story?)

Chapter Seven

——

Based on what we had discovered so far in the hatbox, we could already reconstruct, along general lines, the path Guilhermina had followed in her four years of travel through Europe. A reference in one letter had cleared up a question that interested me from a practical standpoint. After all, I asked myself at each new pirouette of this young aunt, what sort of person was this who circulated on her own from Paris to Agadir among aristocrats, artists, and a procuress with a band of green dwarfs? What keys could have opened so many doors, in so many places, in such a short time?

For although some of the encounters, like that with Paul Nat, Marie-France, or a mysterious telegraph operator called Etienne, had occurred by sheer chance, others, as the hatbox progressively revealed, seemed more orderly, as if the people involved all belonged to the same circle. At any rate, regardless of their origin or quality, all of her adventures assumed a familiarity with cities and customs that a foreigner on her first visit abroad could hardly have acquired without help, especially being so very young and coming from a lost country located at the remotest of peripheries.

The explanation was simple and made sense. Guilhermina

——

had received a card expressing the condolences of the European branch of the Maia Macedo family—to which, after all, she also belonged. Once the sacramental period of mourning was past, she decided to visit her husband's far-flung relatives, thus entering a world that up to then she had only experienced through reading.

Above all, she had made a decision to escape from the plantation, which suddenly oppressed her. Without consulting anyone (she had been estranged from her parents and her only brother for years), she had therefore written to some of these cousins, the Gervoise-Boileau, who had welcomed her in Paris—in the same way that, half a century earlier on the other side of the Apennines, other cousins, the di San Rufos, had received her husband at the castle in Sardone.

So Guilhermina had stayed in the *hôtel particulier* of the Gervoise-Boileau family for two months, and spent two weeks at the family's country home in Normandy, showered with the attentions due a young widowed cousin who also (detail always appreciated by the more affluent) commanded a fortune sufficiently comfortable to do as she liked—and even to permit her to make a few rather daring gestures. (She had presented the Danish aristocrat, of genteel poverty, whom she met at a family dinner, with the balloon in which he later floated out of her life. This gesture cost her no small sum. On another occasion, she had bought from a remote in-law a racehorse which actually ran against obscure competitors at Auteuil, though with little success, before falling victim to a mortal equine fever.)

It was curious to observe, nevertheless, that while this rarified society had made possible certain contacts and opened numerous interesting doors, there remained a large collection of people Guilhermina had frequented during those four years who seemed to have sprung fortuitously from the pavements. It was as if she had prolonged, now in her wanderings through Europe, the same duplicity of her not-so-distant days on the coffee plantation. Thus

---

45

Guilhermina continued to move between two worlds, passing from light to shade with the same speed she had earlier demonstrated in her reading, leaping from one book to another.

Books, which she had devoured in her adolescence and later read with equal intensity (in fact, her only continuing link with her past), explained in themselves another mystery: that of her almost instant success with new friends and lovers. No wonder Paul Nat was surprised to discover that, with the exception of a few more recent authors (Apollinaire and Eluard among them), Guilhermina had read an arsenal of books that was not so different, in quality or quantity, from his own. Furthermore, she had kept abreast of the major trends of her time, in the fields of music, fine arts, and fashion—thanks to the influence of her books and magazines.

She dressed elegantly and discreetly, as her photographs attested, passing now through our hands. It seemed she could converse in an amiable and civilized way—and in quite good French— about an ample range of subjects. Which was a great deal, if we consider the life she had led up to then. Indeed, her European relatives had barely disguised the relief they felt on watching her, that first night at the *hôtel particulier,* correctly dressed and seated at the table, debone a pheasant with obvious dexterity. Any small *faux-pas* that by chance might be noticeable was immediately pardoned and eclipsed by her young, graceful beauty, which had quickly seduced relatives, friends, and servants. *"La petite brésilienne est tout à fait bien,"* the hired help had at once pronounced, an endorsement that had qualified her, like none other in those parts, to take her place at the table, in the sun—and under the sheets of one of the cousins, who never dreamed he would learn so much in such a short time. *"Elle est formidable,"* some said, *délicieuse,* others thought, charmed with various specific aspects of her personality or anatomy.

These conquests in the most varied spheres she owed to her talent and her audacity, but also, in good measure, to Dr. Flávio Eduardo, behind whose thick eyeglasses, for seven decisive years, the vital star of a great master had shone. Much later on, in fact, she would feel comforted by the idea that he had been the only person to know that the death of his friend and cousin had been anything but natural. It seemed poetically just to her that he, who was the principal person responsible for her intellectual formation, had deciphered the culminating scene of her career. Especially since, as was the case, he himself had also played a role in the whole story, however unwilling.

And it was just at this point that Andrea now brought to light, atop one of the little piles before us, the letter in which Flávio Eduardo had disclosed his discovery to her. *Esteemed cousin,* he had begun almost half a century before. The handwriting, uniform and unhurried, was oval and slanted a bit to the right. The black ink had been applied on white paper which now showed perceptible spots of brownish mold. The text, though light enough to seem spontaneous, had probably been carefully thought out. In his fifteen pages, Flávio Eduardo had addressed his theme with the precision of a surgeon, the elegant perspicacity of a disinterested police detective, the grace of a cinematographer with a good eye for detail—all this without omitting moments of genuine emotion.

Barra Mansa, November 13, 1939

Esteemed Cousin,

    You will understand better than anyone else the reasons for my distant behavior toward you since your return from Europe. When I went with you to board the ship five years ago, you wondered at my silence. I promised that one day, perhaps when you returned, I would tell you what was going through my mind at that time. In a way, what I have to say is simple—simple to tell, although the fact itself is not. Many would perhaps even characterize it as monstrous, whether rightly or not—and strictly speaking, it doesn't matter. The fact is—and pardon the unceremonious manner with which I now come to the point—I am personally convinced that Carlos

47

Augusto did not, as we say in these parts, just up and die. Much to the contrary.

Notice that I do not say "poor Carlos Augusto." Knowing you, as I do, dear cousin, I realize that you would not have mobilized so much energy toward an undertaking in itself condemnable before God and Man, if you had not had good reason. Thus I do not judge your actions.

You remember—you foresaw—that, as a doctor, I was the one to examine Carlos Augusto in the wine cellar. A heart attack seemed obvious. The extreme pallor, thinness, and unkempt appearance were surprising. But what most startled me, so much that the memory has stayed with me all through these years, was his right fist, strangely clenched and rigid. You will remember that, as I bathed him in preparation for the funeral— and I will spare you, cousin, my recollection of the fetid vapors he exuded—I almost broke one of his fingers trying to open that right fist. You had gone off to get a second basin of water when I finally pried his hand partially open. And do you know what I found? A small tuft of red hair, which I now return to you.

It is your hair, of course. Put it away carefully, for it has kept me good company. For you, it represents a memory from the past; for me, a last message from a friend. No man dies with a tuft of hair clenched in his fist without good reason.

On that night, once Carlos Augusto was bathed and laid out, I almost put those strands of hair in the pocket of his dark suit coat, behind his white handkerchief. But I decided to keep them in my pocket, in a gesture representing at minimum a promise to keep thinking about what they meant. Because the choice was quite clear: either I was to question his death then, or stay quiet forever.

What would Carlos Augusto's wish have been? To denounce you, probably. But on what level, and with what consequences? A police report involving the family in a scandal? Or a letter that, one day, maybe years later, would say: "Look here, I'm sending you back this tuft of hair." In the end, what really happened? A fight between husband and wife? Strange place for an argument, especially for a man supposedly just out of bed after days of fever and prostration.

I had to know. And so, in the months that followed, again and again I took these strands of hair from the envelope where I kept them, as if looking for inspiration to reconstruct the whole story. Incurable romantic that I am, I brought them along in my pocket the day I took you to board the ship. And it was precisely after you went away that I found energy to probe into the matter more deeply.

As you yourself asked me to do, I went back to the old plantation house from time to time in your absence. And, on the pretext of keeping an eye on the coffee production (declining badly in spite of my efforts) I spoke with people, from the foreman Menezes to the del Vecchio brothers, and naturally with Teresa and Joaquim. I re-created the course of events, imagined situations—I even confess that once, seated on the bottom step of the staircase that leads down to the wine cellar, wiping those old spectacles you know so well, I actually heard strange peals of laughter that seemed to have been caught there, haunted.

I am an old man and have been ill for many years. I mean you no harm whatsoever. For this reason I assure you in advance that this letter will have no consequences; there will be no denunciations or scandals. Your coming marriage to the Portuguese fidalgo, of whom I have heard good reports, is not at all threatened. What matters to me is that you receive this lock of hair safe and sound.

Carlos Augusto passed away toward the end of Holy Week after a prolonged influenza which supposedly kept him bedridden. Yet strangely enough, he died in an almost-empty wine cellar. You told me in tears that he had wished to inspect the remodeling of the wine cellar on the first occasion he got up. But coincidence or not, work on the plantation during that week was almost at a standstill, not just on account of the holidays but also in anticipation of some machinery about to arrive from Europe. Do you remember? There were only two servants there to help you, Teresa and Joaquim. I had the pleasure of hearing from them how zealously you cared for Carlos Augusto throughout his severe influenza.

Well, cousin, you would probably be surprised at the number of small details these servants observed during that Holy Week, though without even remotely grasping the whole picture. It was as if two disciples had witnessed Calvary, and were gaily discussing nails, crosses, sandals, crowns of thorns, drops of blood, Roman tunics, thunder, spears, and yet never once mentioned the Crucifixion. But the vignettes furnished by the servants were no less precious for that reason. In honor of Carlos Augusto and yourself I have tried to piece things together as best I could. If for the sake of analogy I were to use an art form to describe the undertaking, I would say that my afternoons were spent making a collage, like a child discovering the pleasures of freely manipulating scissors, glue, and paper.

Thus, with the patience of someone who had spent not afternoons, but four or five years examining a tiny fragment of history, Flávio Eduardo interviewed participants, revisited places, touched objects, read and reread old letters and receipts, reconstructed walks and conversations, and sat for hours on end to meditate. He had then offered Guilhermina his version of those remote autumn days on the plantation when, after seven years of waiting, knowing the moment had finally arrived, she got her old husband to go down to the cellar and begin the first stage of a journey to hell.

Flávio Eduardo's letter served as a kind of counterpoint to the oral version of the events Guilhermina had left in her niece's custody. Compared to Andrea's tale, the letter was much more precise.

In spite of the care taken to avoid an accusatory tone, it was infused with the need to prove a theory, and hence contained an almost obsessive quantity of details, many of which were totally useless. For instance, it described the colors of the teacups the couple had used prior to the sudden influenza and the number of bucketfuls of hot water carried upstairs for a morning bath. Flávio Eduardo made Joaquim recall the exact position of a sleeping cat, or the way a piece of toast had been bitten into. From Teresa the cook he had collected more smells, colors, and sounds—every imaginable sort of minutiae.

Andrea's version, if less objective, was lighter and in some ways more fun. She told of the amusing bet with Teresa, who banged a spoon against a saucepan and then screamed from down in the wine cellar without Guilhermina being able to hear her from anywhere in the house, once the two doors separating the parlor from the staircase were shut. She mentioned the light-colored out-fit Guilhermina chose so carefully on that autumn day; the straw hat adorning her face; the kiss on the husband's forehead as she woke him on the veranda that faced the orchard. Andrea's version let the observer see, between the lines, the sacred pleasure of a woman about to change her fate.

Dissecting the same scenes, Flávio Eduardo suppressed the shadings of happiness and delicacy for the sake of a more objective account. He traced a straight line, at times cold and severe, between the wife's cunning snare and the husband's unwitting stupor, not noticing that the boundary had instead been sinuous and often sunny, with moments of genuine affection and good humor—tempered, to be sure, with unexpected alarms.

For example, Guilhermina had told Andrea that her husband, discovering he was corralled, had spent a long moment laughing crazily as he rattled the bars, which made her laugh too, harder than she had laughed since the days of her happy childhood. For a short while the two of them had roared with mirth, he pounding the iron grille that separated them, she dancing about, dangling the keys a few feet in front of his face. Until he had lunged for her like a tiger, and had almost thrust her head between the bars. Terrified and breathless, supporting herself against the wall, one hand on her now-tangled hair, keys on the floor, she then realized that, more than bars, what now separated them was the very precision of the roles imposed on them by the scene: he had to die, and she had to kill him. One mistake on her part and the roles would be reversed.

Discounting the small differences between the two accounts, which were more of form than of content, it could be seen that, like harmonic phrases weaving the same melody, they in essence complemented each other, forming a picture that was probably quite faithful to what had actually transpired in those days of pleasure and agony. Guilhermina herself, by telling her niece about Flávio Eduardo's letter, had legitimized its contents—though with a curious restriction. In the didactic tone of a master forced to recognize the merits of an assistant, she said that the images were correct, but reflected her husband's perspective exclusively. Guilhermina was less interested in the specific contents of the letter than in the narrator's point of view, always severely focused on her. Rereading the letter myself, I saw her point. Her husband didn't really stand out clearly. Dr. Flávio Eduardo's words, on the contrary, always kept her in the spotlight as the sole agent in the story. Which was normal enough, since he had no way of knowing what had gone before.

So what we ended up with was, on one side, Guilhermina's version in vibrant color, with the husband illumined by full sunlight or enveloped in suggestive shadows. On the other side we had, by way of Flávio Eduardo, the Honorable's version, in black and white, with the wife elevated to the foreground in somber tones. Ours was the privilege, risky but tempting, to meld colors, planes, and points of view into a conclusive whole.

But it was late, and we went to bed. In separate hammocks, naturally, for such seemed to be my fate. The more agitated the young aunt's life became, the more chaste that of her niece and, by extension, my own.

Chapter Eight

The end of a sunny afternoon. The Honorable Maia Macedo, as is his custom, takes his siesta in one of the rocking chairs on the veranda facing the orchard. He is dreaming. Later on, during one of the phases of his slow death, he will tell Guilhermina about his dream. In spite of the mild temperature, a blanket covers his stomach and a coat his shoulders. On the floor beside his chair are a magazine and some letters from overseas. Usually the volume of correspondence received by the Honorable is small, and for this reason he sometimes takes one or two days to open a letter in order to prolong the pleasure that separates the receiving and the reading of it. This afternoon, however, he opened his letters while he had tea with Guilhermina, for he knew their contents were related to farm matters, a subject about which he was trying to instruct his young wife. Together they discussed the correspondence with Menezes, the foreman, who stood holding his hat as he bade farewell to the couple before leaving for Barra Mansa to spend the holidays at a sister's house, along with his wife, three daughters, and his nieces and nephews.

Enclosed in the letters were copies of receipts for machinery to select and dry coffee beans, recently ordered from Liverpool. The originals had been received and processed at the Rio de

Janeiro customhouse some weeks ago, and the machines were already on their way to the plantation. They would be used during the coming harvest, around the beginning of June.

The foreman took the opportunity to thank Mrs. Macedo for the days of rest on behalf of the laborers. In the course of their conversation, Guilhermina tried to bring up the subject of building a school for the workers' children at the boundary separating their property from cousin Flávio Eduardo's. As usual, whenever the conversation turned to social issues, the Honorable just ate his toast in silence.

Guilhermina then finished her tea and went inside. Before leaving, Menezes reminded the Honorable that the del Vecchio brothers had been put in charge of everyday chores, and would be available if any need should arise. The supplies that had come from the city that morning had already been checked by the mistress herself, who also supervised storing them on the newly built shelves across from the wine cellar. The last bottles had been removed from the wine cellar and the space was now cleared and ready for the remodeling that was to be done. A total of 177 bottles of various types of wines and liqueurs had been counted and stored in the kitchen pantry in spite of Teresa's bad humor over this invasion of her domain. The Honorable and Menezes had a good laugh over Teresa. During the trip upstairs, two bottles had escaped from Joaquim's hands. The Honorable did not seem to mind.

The foreman, on his way out, reiterated his reservations about using the old wine cellar to store the extra parts belonging to the newly purchased machines. In his view, the recent small thefts on the plantation didn't justify the choice of such an awkward place. The Honorable recalled with a sigh his doctor's renewed restrictions on alcohol. What good was a wine cellar to him now? Besides, why not accept his wife's suggestion, since her interest in running the plantation should be encouraged? If the idea didn't work out, they could always put things back as they had been before. Minutes away from his vacation, Menezes didn't insist. Three or four sentences later, he said good-bye.

The Honorable continues to dream. A light breeze now pushes one of the empty envelopes inside the parlor, where Joaquim, kneeling on the polished boards of the floor, is waxing a cupboard with concentration. Lying on a corner of the rug, one of Guilhermina's cats raises its head and watches the envelope, which slides under its eyes until it rests against the can of wax. Joaquim observes the beautiful stamps with their blue and orange profiles of Queen Victoria, and sees that the postmark is from last month, April 1933. He walks out on the veranda and puts the envelope together with the papers under a magazine. He also picks up the tray that is resting on a small table between the chairs and puts the two ivory-colored china cups back in the kitchen, chewing a last bit of toast sprinkled with grated cheese as he goes. The cat falls asleep again.

In the kitchen, Joaquim places the tray on the heavy pine table where Teresa is gutting a chicken, pulling out its yellow insides as the other two cats watch attentively. For some time, the mistress's steps have been audible from the upper floor, their echo moving from one side of the kitchen to the other. The cook registers this noise on the outer limits of consciousness as something familiar but out of context. Normally the mistress isn't so agitated in the afternoon. Only much later, pressured by Flávio Eduardo, was she to recall, smiling, the mischievous thought that passes through her mind now: late-afternoon restlessness, that's what happens when an old man takes a young wife.

Guilhermina finally stops in front of the window and observes the hills planted with coffee which stretch undulating to the limits of the horizon. At this hour of the afternoon, a western breeze blows through her room. It's the time of day when, hearing the distant sound of the workers talking as they return to their huts, she generally closes her book and goes down to have a look at the preparations for dinner.

Guilhermina has the sensation that today the workers are going past her window for the last time. Actually, they will continue walking down the same path for years on end, and their children and grandchildren after them: the workers won't change, but her window will. On the dresser beside her, a mirror reflects her profile. Her eyes are fixed on the landscape before her, thoughts concentrated on a specific item. Guilhermina is thinking about apple pie.

Some time has passed. On the veranda, the Honorable's head rests on his chest, his white hair stirring in the breeze. He snores lightly. In spite of his age, which has slowed him a bit, he continues to be a strong, corpulent man. The cat suddenly jumps up on his lap and he opens his eyes with a start. Guilhermina kisses his forehead contentedly. Teresa and Joaquim cross the patio in the direction of the orchard, baskets on their arms, a ladder over Joaquim's shoulder. Back in Sardone, young Carlos Augusto has just said good-bye to the Baron di San Rufo, who is off for an afternoon's hunting. He extends his hand shyly to Maria Stella, who wants to show him the most secret of all the dungeons. Guilhermina's voice falls on his ears in a soft echo, repeating,

"—inspect my progress?"

. . . *Maria Stella, your perfume, your calmness, as you undress me . . . Your hand moving over my body . . .*

"Carlos, dear, come have a look at my progress."

Progress. What good is progress if I'm at the end of my life? The sun is gone. Another hour, at least another hour until dinnertime.

"What's for dinner tonight?"

All he thinks about is food. From morning to night, now all he cares about is food. He won't take a bath, hardly changes his clothes, doesn't shave. Breakfast, lunch, and dinner, breakfast, lunch, and dinner. . . . He cuts his meat into a thousand pieces, slowly, a thousand pieces . . .

"Chicken pie with rice, and a lettuce salad. I put a bottle of

---

white wine on ice, in case you'd like some. Teresa is making apple pie for dessert." *It's now or never.* "What about our cellar?"

"Oh, let's leave it for tomorrow." *She looks so well in pastel shades and a hat. (Why a hat?) How beautiful my wife is.* "Dr. Geraldo said he'd come by on Tuesday. From now on, you're the one who'll deal with the bank." *How old I've grown. I ache all over . . . apple pie . . .* "I need to go over some figures with you. Here are the copies of the receipts they sent from England. Put them away in that briefcase." *Menezes is right, that cellar is halfway down to hell. Never mind, in the end it's all the same.*

"You ask me to help you with things, and when I do, you don't pay any attention! Or are you too worn out to go down the steps?" *They've been in the orchard two minutes already.*

"Get this cat off my lap. Watch its claws on my shirt, Guilhermina!" *Maria Stella on top of me. My back naked against the damp cold floor. A dream, my chest all scratched . . .*

The stairs going down to the wine cellar were now illumined by electricity. Lazily, stretching its legs, the cat went with the couple to the top of the steps—but Guilhermina pushed it delicately away with her foot and closed the door on its muzzle. Teresa, coming back with her basket of apples, would later stop for an instant in the living room to leave a few apples in the fruit bowl on top of the buffet. She would remember seeing the cat, motionless beside the door that went down to the cellar, as though waiting. She would also note the hat, forgotten on the blue velvet sofa, and register the smell of floor wax in the air. But she couldn't affirm with certainty whether the Honorable was still out on the veranda or not. Judging by the aroma that wafted from the kitchen, her chicken pie was almost on the point of burning.

The peels from the apples were already coming off in the boiling water when Guilhermina burst suddenly into the kitchen to get a tray from the cupboard—and shattered a glass on the floor. She announced that her husband wasn't feeling at all well, and had retired to his room, where he would have supper that night. Teresa, gathering up the shards of glass on her knees, had asked if he was running a fever. Guilhermina answered that he was, but probably rest would take care of the problem. If not, she would send one of the del Vecchio brothers to fetch Dr. Flávio Eduardo the next morning.

So as not to worry Mrs. Macedo unnecessarily, Teresa chose not to remind her that Dr. Flávio Eduardo was spending Easter week with his daughter and grandchildren in Rio de Janeiro. Guilhermina seemed tense and somewhat worried, her hair disheveled. But there was also a tone of nervous happiness in her voice, as if the Honorable having a cold justified a little more fully her existence as nurse and guardian.

That was Wednesday. From that time on, for the next four days, Mrs. Macedo had taken up her husband's three meals every day on that very same tray, which was invariably brought back a few hours later by the servants from the floor of the hallway beside the door. (Guilhermina herself hardly touched the food Teresa served her in the kitchen.) The Honorable's room was aired and tidied every morning, taking advantage of the time when the mistress, in the bathroom nearby, helped her husband bathe and shave.

The old Honorable was quite docile about letting his wife bathe him, as Joaquim attested; he had heard her soft laughter, along with the sound of water being poured from the large pitchers. Teresa, also, when she went to get one of the trays, had heard the mistress reading aloud to her husband, and the inflection of her voice had been lively, the characters interpreted faithfully, as though she were acting out the scenes. All in all, Teresa and Joaquim pronounced, Maia Macedo didn't realize how lucky he was. There were lots of dedicated wives, but how many, saddled with a sick old husband, when they themselves were in the first flower of youth, would demonstrate such goodwill, competence, and cheerfulness?

The hysterical peals of laughter resounding in the wine cellar on that Wednesday had beaten unheard against the doors that separated it from the rest of the plantation house. But their muffled echoes were still vibrating on the shadowy staircase when Guilhermina, hair falling loose over her torn blouse, gasping as she leaned against the banister, finally saw before her eyes the scene she had imagined for so many years.

Just as in the vision, her husband was almost too big for the frame surrounding him, his hands nearly touching the walls. But the finished picture was inferior to the seven years' sketches, because the man now ranted and raved, shaking the iron bars and chain, in glaring contrast to the silence of the vision.

In less than a minute the Honorable had made the transition from surprise to attack, and produced terrible noises and great clumsy gestures. Where did that old man get so much physical and mental agility? And how did he decode in a flash what had spent seven years in gestation? Guilhermina, running her hands over her own neck as the incomprehensible sounds penetrated her ears, slowly perceived that now that the time had come, it was the nightmares—the famous nightmares her husband had been having for years—that had given him the alert.

But the time for what? the Honorable screamed from the other side of the bars. What the hell was happening? Why didn't he wake up? Why, no matter how hard he shook them, didn't those iron bars dissolve, as they always had, into sheets and blankets?

The Honorable had to know. And Guilhermina, who had spent seven years designing her plan with a delicate paintbrush on porcelain, testing and discarding variables against constantly changing backdrops, realized that she had foreseen nothing of the chapters that she was now about to share with her husband. Thus, she was free to do anything. She could, for instance, refuse to answer the questions he alternately screamed or murmured to her. She could laugh or be serious. She could, supreme of all delights, go back to her childhood and make faces at him.

Or, she could turn out the lights. Turn out the lights just as, exactly seven years before, an oil lamp had been blown out to usher in a night of blood and terror. So there they stood for several long minutes, facing each other, in utter darkness and gradually in utter silence. A silence from which Guilhermina, still blinking in the sudden daylight, was only to emerge when the glass shattered against the tiles of the kitchen floor.

Chapter Nine

Guilhermina made five visits to the wine cellar to monitor her husband's final agony, always between midnight and 4:00 A.M. But at no time was she so strongly impressed as in that initial moment of darkness and silence, when she re-experienced, inverted now as if by a mirror, that long-ago night of helplessness and terror. *Fourteen was a dreadfully early age at which to know so much and be so powerless,* she was to read, years later, in a book that had not yet been written.

Infinite perspectives were suddenly within her reach, a whole new range of opportunities for a young, affluent woman. But for him, the oscillation between anxiety and panic, added to a general sense of abandon and disorientation, were the prelude to a journey toward the limits of the universe. She was moved to feel her husband palpitate at her side almost like a young bird about to begin its flight. He was bound, thanks to her, toward the infinite.

After the interlude of complete darkness, Guilhermina had disappeared as if by magic—and the Honorable had been left alone behind the iron grille, eyes fixed (as he was to tell his wife later) on the crack of light at the bottom of the door. That light coming through its minuscule opening constituted proof that the universe existed. Even when it was turned off, as happened soon afterward, it could be brought back again by the switch of his memory. The Honorable had screamed a few more times, but he soon realized the uselessness of this effort. Little by little, he regained his calm and from that time on showed behavior more in line with what his wife had originally imagined. As a prisoner, he at once deduced that he would not come out of the cellar alive. As a man, he felt swallowed up by a devastating tiredness, as though he suddenly understood that he had based his existence on a great mistake.

At some point in his life something had happened. Now he was here in the dark. In truth (and he smiled bitterly to himself) he was being punished. Except that, like most children, he had no idea what for. But unlike a child, it was his ignorance—and not fear or anger—that stupefied him. He felt like a picture which, without being properly cataloged or with absurdly incomplete annotations, was about to be glued forever into some family album filled with countless pages, and then put on some shelf beside hundreds of other albums in the middle of thousands of other shelves, integrated into an immense library, lost in the infinity of the universe. He wasn't afraid of death, but of labyrinths. Since the time he met the Baroness he had never been afraid of the dark; he was simply insecure. *"Burn the books and the libraries and bring in the musicians, because there's no time to spare!"* he was to yell deliriously to Guilhermina during his last hours.

According to the servants, Guilhermina had imposed a concise routine on herself during those five days. In the morning she helped her husband to wash, shave, and freshen up because, as she told Teresa, the high fever wasn't going down as fast as she expected. Later, after the room had been aired and the bed made, she went down personally to fetch their breakfast, which she ate with her husband. After that they would talk, or she would read aloud to him. So the Honorable could rest more peacefully in his room, she kept the curtains half-closed, and spent the rest of the morning accompanying the work of Teresa and Joaquim in the parlor or the kitchen, talking with them perhaps a bit more than usual.

After their interviews with Flávio Eduardo (in the months that followed Guilhermina's departure for Europe) the servants realized that they had never actually heard the Honorable's voice answering his wife's words or laughter. They also recollected that the mistress hadn't set foot outside the house in those five days, not even for her habitual walks through the gardens. No, it hadn't been raining. On the contrary, the weather had been beautiful. On at least two occasions one of the del Vecchio brothers had brushed and saddled the mistress's favorite horse and tied it to the porch rail, but the animal remained there without so much as a lump of sugar in gratitude.

At midday, after taking her husband his lunch, Guilhermina would come down to have a meal herself. Though these meals were light, she left them virtually untouched on her plate. (After all, she told her niece with an amused wink, she had just polished off the lunch supposedly intended for her husband in the bedroom upstairs, with excellent appetite. It was the simplest and most natural way to make it disappear.) Then, when she wasn't watching over her patient, she spent her afternoons reading or doing embroidery. Yes, she invariably stayed in the parlor, the three cats at her feet, sitting on the same sofa in front of the staircase that led to the bedrooms on the second floor, beneath which was the door that went to the cellar and the iron-barred storeroom. As she was in the habit of reading on the veranda, or in the little office adjacent to the parlor or in her bedroom, the servants supposed that this change reflected her zeal to stay near her husband in case he might need her. Flávio Eduardo, however, had raised an additional hypothesis, for as he said in his letter,

> ". . . a superficial examination of the parlor's dimensions in relation to the cellar would allow one to affirm beyond the shadow of a doubt, that the sofa on which you were reading Madame Bovary, cousin, was situated precisely above

the wine cellar and therefore just above Carlos Augusto's
head . . ."

which seemed to him in bad taste and *vaguely diabolical,* although he
didn't rule out, a few lines further on, *the possibility of a coincidence.*
Guilhermina, who had remarked to Andrea on that particular suspicion of Flávio Eduardo's, had chuckled at this accusation, for she
too had realized the coincidence with a small shiver. But according
to her, the servants were wrong on one point (or Flávio Eduardo
had permitted himself an unfounded analogy), since she had spent
those days of her husband's expiration reading the correspondence
of George Sand and Padre Vieira's *Sermons,* and not Flaubert.

As though adding a footnote to her story, she reiterated to her
niece that in no way did she nourish a macabre hatred for her
husband. On the contrary, for a long while the old Honorable,
divested of his claws and his swagger, had to be stirred in her imagination to stay alive, like coals about to go out in a fireplace.

The Honorable, in fact, had long since been reduced to a
project, the roots of which were now almost lost in her past. Although his death continued to be her reason to live, the desire for
revenge was virtually gone. Particularly because, as the years passed
by, Guilhermina came to realize that her husband had not acted in
bad faith by raping her the way he had. Indeed, on one level, she
had actually forgiven him. And because she forgave him she felt
free, on another level, to sacrifice him unmercifully in a sort of
purifying ritual that would permit her to regain control of her own
life and determine the direction it would take. *"It wasn't my fault,
nor was it his."* she told her niece enigmatically. *"The levels were to
blame."*

This comment, made by chance, had caused Andrea to ask
herself if her great-aunt, to all appearances a normal person—indeed, a master at demonstrating this apparent normality all through
her adult life—might not have experienced a specific period of in-
sanity with her husband. A Guilhermina who draped herself in her

red-and-white sheet and chopped her husband to pieces with an ax in the midnight hours of their wedding night would star in a lamentable scene, but one to some extent comprehensible and, for many, even praiseworthy. But her case was different. With the precision of a surgeon who microscopically delimits his field of operation, Guilhermina seemed to have been rigorously selective in the demarcation of her madness, to the point of conferring on it a rudimentary base of philosophical support.

Seeing in a new light the serene-faced old lady before her, vestiges of beauty still evident behind the delicate wrinkles, Andrea decided to probe more deeply into that space delineated by such subtle boundaries. She had asked her aunt if killing her husband didn't constitute, in her view, an act worthy of more severe judgment.

As Guilhermina seemed not to have heard, and began to sing softly to her cat (a direct descendant of those cats which, fifty years before, had walked on rugs that lay ten yards above her dying husband's head), the niece framed the question in more precise terms. She asked if locking the husband up for five days until he finally died of a heart attack provoked by hunger and neglect didn't seem to her an extremely refined act of cruelty. At which the aunt, as though sensitive to the worries of a niece whose curiosity for mysteries should not be discouraged, murmured softly,

"Do you really think so?"

Then she had been silent for a few minutes, lost in deep reflection. Andrea had respected her silence. And if I know Andrea, she had wiped all traces of shock from her face. After a little while, her aunt, in a sudden impulse, as if remembering some important detail, rewarded her patience. In the tone one uses to add an additional point to an argument, however unnecessarily, she said,

"You know, dear, I myself took care to ask him that. The part about the cruelty. And he assured me it wasn't so. Not at all. He even smiled at me, from the floor."

"From the floor? When was that?" Andrea insisted.

"Toward the very end," her aunt replied.

Between this final dialogue with the Honorable gasping his last breaths on the floor, and the first conversations, in the hours after midnight on Thursday morning, the two had communicated like never before. If she hadn't been so taken up with killing him, they might actually have become friends. "I would have loved him, if I had not killed him," she told her niece.

Andrea, aware of the importance of those five days, had then removed her trappings of niece and behaved like a reporter with a master's degree in sociology. Without tiring or pressuring Guilhermina, she made her aunt repeat verbatim those midnight conversations in the cellar of a plantation house lost in the interior of Brazil in the year 1933. She rescued entire speeches and, more than that, their probable order of occurrence and the silences that gave them rhythm and meaning. For Andrea, who only later would have access to the hatbox, these conversations had epitomized the whole story.

But it was for Flávio Eduardo, like the good doctor and wise man that he was, to see that what had happened was not a death, but a rebirth. Summoned urgently by the younger del Vecchio brother, and still wearing the clothes in which he had journeyed from Rio, he rushed down the cellar steps—but was arrested at the bottom, behind the half-open door, his asthma medicine in his hand. And before he saw the woman seated on the floor, stroking her husband's head, even before taking a handkerchief out of his pocket, stunned by the *fetid vapors* that quickly invaded his nostrils, he had heard, deeply moved,

"*. . . your voice, cousin, singing very softly and with infinite sweetness, the most beautiful lullaby I ever heard in all my life . . .*"

Guilhermina also mentioned that scene. She told Andrea that it was the same lullaby she always sang to her dolls when she put them to sleep. She was taking up her life again at the point where it had been interrupted.

Chapter Ten

Almost without realizing it, Andrea and I were starting our third day on the farm, ever more immersed in Guilhermina's adventures. We tacitly agreed to stay on. It was vacation time and nothing called me back to the university. Andrea had an assistant to run the Night Stand, since she went on frequent buying trips to Rio or São Paulo to look for antiques, and often came here simply to rest. Besides, there were the swims in the waterfall, the kitchen with its wood-burning stove, the unpredictable hatbox revealing its secrets little by little, the pleasant temperature, the lazy conversations with the caretaker and his wife, the night in our hammocks under the stars—in short, nothing encouraged a quick return to the city. Also, Andrea and I were starting to take tender winding walks through the hills around the farmhouse, holding each other by the waist or hand in hand in a turn-of-the-century courtship. In its glow we continued delicately to unfold new aspects of Guilhermina's story. Without telling her, I had already begun to make a few notes on paper, in a shy prelude to an eventual script, which would probably join older and dustier siblings someday in my generous bottom drawer.

Once again, on that third sunny morning, we had been awakened by the singing of the birds, mixed with the laughter of the caretaker's children playing nearby. As we lounged in our hammocks, glasses of fresh orange juice in our hands, a new rooster took his place on the swing, glancing uneasily around him as though looking for his predecessor, walking the eternal tightrope between audacity and prudence. With Guilhermina perched in my memory, I thought how much I would have liked to hear her wonderful story, not on the farm where she had spent her last days, but on the plantation where that story had begun.

After more than fifty years, would the old mansion in the state of Rio de Janeiro still be standing? What would it be like? We had a few glimpses available thanks to two or three eyewitnesses, but no systematic description. We hadn't found any pictures of the coffee plantation in the hatbox. But it wasn't hard to reconstruct the approximate scenery against which the events had been played out.

The house, more the permanent residence of a man of wealth than a mere farmhouse, must have been imposing. During the Honorable's life, he had probably inherited furniture, dinnerware, and fine objects from his wealthy and aristocratic family, forming a collection that he had augmented on his trips abroad, the vestiges of which were still to be seen in the Night Stand. Subsequent to that initial European trip at age twenty, Maia Macedo had returned there on two occasions (once on an early zeppelin flight) and had also made, with his first wife, a honeymoon trip to Argentina and Uruguay. Between what he had inherited and what he acquired, one would suppose the house was well appointed, large, and comfortable, one of those majestic rural properties that the coffee barons had maintained in the first half of the nineteenth century all through the Paraíba Valley.

We were certain that the house had two floors, the ground floor with a veranda at the front looking out onto the orchard, a spacious parlor, an office (which in earlier days had probably housed an oratorium), and a dining room. On the other side of the parlor, in the wing opposite the veranda, was a hallway, probably leading to a guest bathroom and to the kitchen, also large and airy, with blue tiles similar to those we appreciated now as we warmed our coffee.

We spent considerable time trying to situate, in the parlor of that mansion, the staircase that went up to the second floor, beneath which we knew was located the door that opened onto the cellar steps. Imagining a large rectangular room and placing ourselves on the side of the veranda, our backs to the orchard, we finally put the staircase diagonally across the room, against the wall on the extreme opposite side. We decided it probably rose from left to right since we had placed the hallway leading to the kitchen on the right side. Beyond the kitchen was the service area with its washbasins, clotheslines, and servants' quarters.

Going up the staircase we again viewed the watercolors by Ender and Hildebrandt, hung between two oil paintings by Bertichen, and arrived at a hallway off which four or five bedrooms must have been—one of them no doubt transformed into a sewing room. The bathroom was probably at the end of the hall, with its windows opening to the side of the house.

Guilhermina's room (at some point she had established a *chambre à part*) was on the right, directly above the kitchen, opposite Maia Macedo's room, which therefore had to be located on the left, above part of the parlor and the veranda. We had no doubt as to which direction Guilhermina's room faced, because her windows looked out over the coffee plantation, on the side opposite the orchard, and her steps were heard by Teresa in the kitchen below.

We imagined that Maia Macedo's quarters, which we knew included a private bath, were larger and must have corresponded approximately to the size of the parlor. Taking the staircase as a reference, the other two or three bedrooms probably were farther down the hall. Used by infrequent guests (Andrea didn't remember any mention of a social life that included prolonged stays of visitors), these rooms had no doubt been intended for the children the Honorable never had.

Here Andrea gave a start, clapping her hand to her forehead as she recalled that her aunt had told her that Teresa, the cook, once made a cryptic reference to a bastard son of Macedo's. The child had been born a few years before the Honorable's first marriage (to the fat woman who had drowned during the picnic), the fruit of one of the countless adventures he had permitted himself with the farm laborers' wives or daughters. This time, the affair involved the oldest daughter of the previous foreman. Neither the Honorable, nor Teresa, nor Joaquim, nor any of the other employees had ever known this boy (whose age was probably close to Guilhermina's) because the foreman, in exchange for silence and compliance, had been given the means to install himself on a little plot of land near the border of Mato Grosso and São Paulo, and moved there with his family a few months before the illegitimate child was born. Presumably the Honorable never even knew he had a son, a secret that Dr. Flávio Eduardo (who had been the intermediary in the transactions and had kept in touch with the foreman's family) had let slip one day in a moment of apparent absentmindedness.

Although irrelevant to the story of Guilhermina and her husband, the news that there existed a little Maia Macedo in the interior of São Paulo State (almost eighty years old, if he was alive), or of possible descendants scattered through the countryside, was gratifying to me, though I couldn't say why. It was rather as if the absence of direct descendants of the story's protagonists bothered me somehow. I liked the idea that, somewhere on this planet, and maybe closer than I imagined, a great-grandchild of the man who had made love to the Baroness di San Rufo a century ago might be, at that moment, playing marbles with a friend, like the caretaker's children outside.

If one were to search through the papers of the old plantation, if they still existed, or among the public records of the old district of Barra Mansa, where he would have been born, maybe one might unearth the name of that employee who had become a grandfather against his will, and from there begin combing through the counties of São Paulo State that bordered Mato Grosso. But to what end? To tell some old man that another old man, his remote father, had died of hunger and thirst locked up in a cellar? No, Andrea's sudden recollection was more interesting as a symbol than as a fact. A window had opened, it didn't matter onto what.

In the sequence of these memories, Andrea remembered Guilhermina once telling her that she had spent a substantial portion of her time as Macedo's wife sitting before the window of her room, simply looking out, as if contemplating a painting. As in the case of the little Maia Macedo, who evaporated out of one place to materialize in some other, window and canvas became interchangeable. Moreover, as she was to learn in the most beautiful of her books, a window, in provincial places, substitutes for theaters and outings. Thus, when she wasn't wandering through the universe of her books or perfecting her trap by observing her husband, or busy with her duties as mistress of a plantation, Guilhermina lost herself in the contemplation of other worlds. She would blend her husband's journeys, which he continued to describe to her, with the fields that stretched away beyond the little stream, with the colors that changed with the changing hours, with the men who returned from their day's work, or the cattle being driven from one pasture to another. Intermingled with these images she traced others of the landscapes she was yet to visit, where she would meet people similar to the characters in her novels, legends, and poems. She dreamed, then, about Montparnasse and the sidewalks where she would pause one summer afternoon to look at two drawings by Miró, about whom she had just read a fascinating article. How was it possible to paint like that?

Part Two

Chapter Eleven

————

When Fernando asked me to write Guilhermina's story down, I was somewhat at a loss. Not that writing was a problem; I've worked for magazines, written for newspapers—no, the problem was of a different nature. I didn't feel right telling Fernando everything, or everything in full detail, that Guilhermina revealed to me during my visits to her farm in Goiás. Actually, I never imagined at first that I would talk to him much about Guilhermina. Four years previously, when I met her, I had decided that Guilhermina was my own business, part of a personal heritage that it was my duty to protect and preserve from invasions. I had a series of reasons, some easy to explain, others hard. First of all, I didn't want to make my great-aunt into a soap opera. Not only was it a question of personal fidelity to her memory, but my parents, aunts, and uncles are all very much alive, and the publicity generated would probably shed an unfavorable light on my family. Second because, due to bashfulness or lack of clarity, I wanted to form my own conclusions regarding Guilhermina and her story—a possibility that was threatened when, eighteen months after her death, Fernando one day stumbled into the Night Stand and fell into my arms.

Meeting Fernando again plunged me suddenly back into a

————

very meaningful time in my past, a period of movements and breakups, my departure from a politically closed Brazil, my discovery of California and its spaces, Murilo, Jung, Watergate, and the temptation to be an actress. Perhaps that's why, when Fernando asked me about the origin of the Night Stand's name, I started talking about Guilhermina without even realizing it, so naturally that I was startled to find myself well along in the story. Later, in Fernando's candlelit apartment, I heard myself talking in the shadows, the words forming sentences like wool being spun into thread on a spindle. I was pleased at this, like an author faithful to his character, who accurately reproduces what he has heard. It was the first time I had really talked about Guilhermina. Up to then, not even my best friends or my two ex-husbands had been aware of her story. They knew a few fragments—enough to justify my moving to Brasília, opening an antique shop, and visiting a farm in Goiás from time to time.

Anyway, I told Fernando the story—at least its general outline. Not that I omitted much (the Marie-France episode, for example, I didn't know about myself). But from there to writing it all down in detailed order, and helping make it into a script, is a distance I don't intend to go. Furthermore, besides the reasons I already mentioned, I have severe doubts about Fernando's abilities as a scriptwriter. I know I'm getting into an extremely sensitive personal area here; Fernando is a wonderful person, talented, a great cook, but the truth is, I don't know if he's up to dealing with anything of a very large scope. *Murder in the Springtime,* his only film, was riddled with problems, confused, poorly conceived, and almost boring. If he had made a bad film, realized it, and accepted the fact, I would still have some hope for his future in that area. But it alarmed me at the time to realize that in his mind, *Murder* wasn't hailed as a masterpiece simply because of secondary production-related details. True, its budget was modest, almost do-it-yourself.

Of course, ten years have passed and during that time we've all lived and learned a good deal. Swept along (or pushed) by Fernando's enthusiasm and by the revelations from the hatbox—which, in truth, whetted my curiosity considerably—I ended up taking a major part in the project. My mistake was telling Fernando about the hatbox before going through it carefully myself. Never mind. At any rate, it's one thing to talk and another thing to write. Hence my problem: I feel some personal discomfort in coming up with a text based on the story, as if, after crossing forbidden barriers, I were now being compelled to move ahead against my own will.

But Fernando, I'm forced to recognize, has a special way of insisting. He is very patient and knows how to exploit other people's weak spots with ability. He explained that he only needed a small text that would serve to help him out with his eventual script, and that it was one thing to talk, recollecting things out of order and without obligation, and another to put it all in order and write it down. He said this while we were still on the farm, the day before we returned to Brasília after almost a week's absence, when we were naked under the waterfall and he finally embraced me. (It took him a while to work up to it, but finally he did.) Later, lying on the grass, I lit a cigarette and went back to his request. I said that very frankly I had no idea where to start. "Any time, any place," he answered, kissing again and again an old tattoo that I have between my breasts. Then he said, "Write twenty pages without rereading them, and don't tear them up before you show them to me."

I've already written at least a hundred, which I reread more than once, and I still don't know if what I wrote will help. The hardest part turned out to be the beginning, which I am thinking of tearing up and throwing away because it has no bearing on Guilhermina's story. I wrote about the period when I met Fernando and his friends and we made that film together. *Murder* was a comedy. I spent six hours in a bathtub to film two takes. I never thought I'd suffer so much making a comedy. The water was freezing, and Murilo, my ex-husband, stuck to us like glue the whole time, and wouldn't believe (as Fernando insisted) that my bare breasts and the blue crab were a metaphor for freedom. "Metaphor, hell! That guy just wants to look at your tits! And then show them to his friends!'' he would mutter furiously in my ear between takes, angry at me, at the film and, of course, at his own jealousy. But I liked Murilo and to this day think of him with affection. In 1974, hiding your wife's breasts from other men's eyes was an acceptable foolishness.

Los Angeles was, indeed, one of the beginnings. Many years later, when I started to do fashion photography and got involved with the creative process again, I thought fondly about those film episodes and that era when we lived in the apartment on Venice Beach—the barbecues on the little porch, my dog Jung wagging his tail and scaring the flies off the meat, our neighbor John, who always had three TV sets on, tuned to different channels (Watergate, Vietnam, and Mickey Mouse) coming and going in our apartment and steadily cursing at the police helicopters that flew over the roofs to see who was planting marijuana in the backyard. "The pigs, the pigs!" he would yell. There were other Brazilians besides Fernando living there at the time, mostly would-be movie stars or just expatriates struggling to survive and of whom I later lost track.

I didn't even see Fernando for ten years, from 1975 to now, when he appeared in the Night Stand. I recognized him easily, though he had gained quite a bit of weight and shaved off his beard. We hugged long and hard; it was good to see him. It was so funny watching his face fall when I pretended not to remember our film. The name of my character was Tallulah, in honor of a great actress of the forties, Tallulah Bankhead, forgotten today, but I was supposed to imitate Lauren Bacall in *To Have and Have Not,* which Fernando made me watch about six times in the old Fox Venice Theater on Lincoln. If Guilhermina's story should become a film someday it will be hard to direct the actress who plays her part, hard to find the right tone. It's complicated to explain, but she communicated things in an oblique way; and when I realized what I was hearing it was almost too late. From then on I would always be one step behind the story, never exactly *inside* it. That's why writing or transcribing what I heard won't help much, because there are some

---

78

stories in which the listener travels along with the narrator, and others in which he stays behind, listen closely as he will. With Guilhermina, once the initial shock was past, it was hard to keep up. I sometimes felt like an outsider, almost an observer. Fernando realized this.

But I don't want to give the impression that Guilhermina deliberately tried to shock me. In a certain sense it is possible that we were both taken by surprise, as if the story, pulsing with a life of its own, had suddenly jumped out at us. I at least felt rather sleepy and wasn't paying much attention that day after lunch, on my second or third visit to her farm, as I listened to her describe the plantations in the Paraíba Valley, using words like *corncrib* and *granary*, recalling grades of coffee and breeds of cattle, and names of patron saints for whom the properties were named, like Santa Luzia, Santana, São Luis da Boa Sorte, when she branched off to describe the plantation houses she had seen in her youth. She explained that there had always been a social area for guests, a private area where the family lived, and a work area for the domestics, but that, in the case of the house where she had spent her married years, there had also been an underground passage—and here, as if taken by a sudden impulse, she placed her face close to mine and added in a whisper—*"with an ancient wine cellar where one day I locked your old grandfather up to die."* This was followed by a pause and the offer of a last biscuit, which I refused. I kept on swinging back and forth in my hammock, asking myself if I had heard right, or if I was supposed to offer some reply. But before I could open my mouth she insisted, her eyes staring into mine: *"Of hunger. And thirst. I starved him to death."* Then, throwing her head back, she ate the last biscuit herself.

"But Auntie," I asked, intrigued, "which grandfather? None of my grandparents died of hunger." Then she shuddered, as if awakening from a dream, and straightened herself up in her chair, scaring the cat. Somewhere in the jumble of memories and landscapes from her childhood, she who from the age of fourteen had planned things so as never to be taken by surprise again, had seemingly confused her first husband with her brother (my paternal grandfather) and thus entered on an oblique angle into one of the most secret compartments of her past.

But this I was only to discover months later, on another visit to the farm, when she finally went back to the story and told it from the beginning. On that night she merely said,

"Excuse me." And more softly, almost into the ear of the cat, which was closing its eyes again, "I made a mistake."

Later on, thinking again about that conversation on my own, I realized that Guilhermina, who had never forgiven my grandfather for doing nothing to prevent the negotiated marriage, had actually conveyed two messages at the same time. Thus, through an apparent slip, she had not only catapulted me into the middle of her tale, but had also pointed out one of those guilty by omission—her brother. Perhaps because she didn't dare to question her parents, she had hoped for some gesture of protest from him in her defense.

Certainly there was a story ahead of me. But one that required very close attention.

Chapter Twelve

I met Guilhermina in 1981. In the ophthalmologist's waiting room where our encounter took place thanks to a receptionist, we talked for only ten minutes. Then she went in for her consultation. When I finished with mine, I found her still waiting, and we went gaily off to a tearoom, like a grandmother and granddaughter out on a shopping spree. Once we were seated and looking over the cakes and biscuits before us, she began to tell me how, years before, she had met Joaquim Guilherme, whom Flávio Eduardo had called *the Portuguese fidalgo* in his letter, in just such a tearoom. That was how she started talking about herself, telling of the cakes and biscuits that had led to her second wedding. Recently arrived after four years in Europe, Guilhermina was having tea at the Colombo Tearoom as she reflected on her future. Her alternatives were to go back to the plantation where she had lived before, or buy a house in the Botafogo neighborhood and move to Rio de Janeiro.

At a table to one side of her, she told me, a man was observing her attentively as he ate his cake. They exchanged a few words about the weather. Joaquim Guilherme was to tell her afterward that he had amazed himself with his courage, for he was not a man given to conquests. But, charmed with the poise and naturalness with which Guilhermina received his comments, he had walked with her to the tramway stop, and jumped up on the back step of the car at the last minute. When he discovered where she was staying, he haunted the vicinity until he could summon up the courage to speak to her again, blushing. As for Guilhermina, she had fanned herself energetically as she gave him to understand she was a widow.

What had attracted Guilhermina to him, besides his being head over heels in love with her, was the certainty that this successful middle-aged businessman, single by choice or through timidity, founding member of the Vasco da Gama Sports Club and a future Rotarian, belonged to another world that had no link whatsoever with her past. "He was a man," she said to me once, "incapable of even dreaming of what I had lived through." She thus sensed that the possibility of her inner world being invaded was remote. Not that she wished to hide anything out of mere anxiety. She simply had not met, nor would she ever meet, a man able to comprehend her cargo of secrets.

A handsome man of modest origins, the Portuguese *fidalgo* was actually a Brazilian, the son of Portuguese immigrants who had come to Brazil at the end of the last century. From them he had inherited some money with which he established, working hard and sacrificing, two small textile factories in the interior of São Paulo State. In the last few years, however, he had turned the operation of these factories over to his younger brothers and moved to Rio, where he hoped to set up outlets for his products, thus avoiding the middlemen who, in São Paulo, were eating into his profits.

With this simple man, "big and full of firm white flesh," good-humored, flower in his lapel, two gold molars and no imagination, Guilhermina wanted to have lots of children as soon as possible. She didn't have them, but with two small exceptions (which she later characterized as "small weaknesses without consequence"), she led a calm, well-behaved life. She was surprised or alarmed only once, when she ran into Paul Nat at Cinelândia.

Coming from Buenos Aires, where he had given a concert, he had landed in Mauá Square that morning and was strolling nonchalantly through the center of the city, fanning himself with his panama hat and carrying an enormous maraca in his hip pocket.

Guilhermina was walking on her husband's arm. Her surprise, though enormous, in the end caused no ill feeling, such was the radiant and fraternal sincerity with which Paul Nat had greeted her. The pianist, with his enthusiasm and foreign mannerisms, had made a genial impression on Joaquim Guilherme. "What an interesting fellow, your friend," he had commented after they said good-bye. (*"Au revoir, ma belle déesse,"* Paul Nat had whispered in Guilhermina's left ear.)

Guilhermina and her husband installed themselves in a beautiful house in the middle of a large lot in Mariz e Barros Street, in Tijuca, where they lived for almost thirteen years, up to the beginning of the fifties, when she was widowed a second time. Little by little she brought to this house most of the furniture, porcelain, art objects, and books from her coffee plantation in the state of Rio. The plantation itself, already starting to decline at the end of the Honorable's life, had not withstood the attempts at modernization which coincided with Guilhermina's four years of European travel, and thus was sold shortly after her second marriage.

Facing me, Guilhermina interrupts her story to stare at me tenderly in silence. She seems to be working up courage to ask me, finally, about my grandfather.

"He died ten years ago."

"I know."

She wants to know what he was like, how he turned out, whom he married, if he had been a good grandfather, what my parents were like, what professions people took up in my family, and what had happened to the famous lands in Barra Mansa received as a consequence of her marriage to the Honorable Maia Macedo. Once the dike has burst, she suddenly wants to know everything—but there's no time, I have a meeting with my divorce lawyer. On impulse, I ask Guilhermina if she has ever eaten sushi. She recovers her smile and, that night, we meet again at Honjin's in São João Batista Street.

When I think of her as she was that night in the Japanese restaurant, I have to make an effort to associate that image—and, more remotely, the image of the young widow recently arrived from Europe who went to the Colombo for tea—to the Guilhermina I discovered later on. Fernando, who only saw photos of her and all taken when she was young, asked me once if I could still see clear traces of beauty in her face. I particularly remember her eyes, now like lenses open to the world, now like curtains shrouding her secrets. I remember the energy and sense of humor she radiated. That night at Honjin's, she had trouble eating with chopsticks, cried copious tears under the impact of the horseradish, and thrust her nose unhesitatingly over the platter to smell the fish.

I also think how strangely restful it must have been, for that Guilhermina newly returned to Brazil in 1938 or 1939, that meeting in the Colombo with her *fidalgo*. What a contrast to the Gervoise-Boileau, whom we knew better now, to Paul Nat and his passionate letters, to Marie-France and her green dwarfs, to Etienne the telegraph operator and his fishing expeditions on the banks of the Marne ("a man who possessed exactly two pairs of pants, two shirts, and a bicycle"), and to so many other things we had discovered in successive excavations through the hatbox, between our plunges beneath the waterfall and our nights in the hammocks.

Things that, in turn, had followed the seven years of her first marriage and all that had occurred in the cellar of the plantation house. For that reason, today, when I observe couples of a certain age eating an ice-cream cone, arm in arm on some sidewalk, I always imagine depths, worlds. How many mysteries hidden behind *"another bite, my dear?" "No, thank you, love. . . ."* How many silks and laces rent amid smoke and train whistles, screams of pleasure or of pain? How many fears caused by a suitcase unexpectedly opened by the police at a border crossing? How many *Tomates Clamart,* how many indignant skeletons, enigmas, omissions . . . ?

Still, if Guilhermina's life had been tumultuous, nothing prevented the man she met at the Colombo from hiding a few secrets of his own. But who would ever know? Guilhermina, perhaps anticipating her new husband's curiosity, had limited her own questions to the essential minimum. Joaquim Guilherme had respected that tacit accord, perhaps convinced that the child-widow's time in Europe had been spent recovering from unspeakable grief. He preferred to imagine that benevolent gods had blown to the table at his side, in an ethereal ship of billowing sails, a chaste wife, the young and immaculate widow of an old and respectful husband. And he attributed her growing enthusiasm in bed to his own talent, failing only to understand precisely why no woman had, up to then, responded to his prowess with such vocal enthusiasm.

And so of the Portuguese nobleman, who was neither Portuguese nor nobleman, almost nothing is left, except his reverent love for his wife, his two gold molars, his shyness contrasting with his solid build, and the carnation in his lapel. Which is a shame, because today, seeing the story as a whole, I believe he might have been rather interesting. Still, it's more likely that he intrigues me only because of Guilhermina, thus confirming the old rule that banal people become interesting by reflecting the brilliance of others. The *fidalgo* was probably worth more by virtue of his obscurity. It's hard to say.

At Honjin's, Guilhermina suggested that I come visit her at her farm in Goiás someday, an idea I found attractive, because living in Rio was becoming a burden for me at the time. I went to the farm eight or ten times, I don't remember exactly, in the course of two years, and our conversations continued until her death. I was in São Paulo, where I had gone to buy some antiques, when Guilhermina died of a heart attack in her sleep. I wasn't even there for the funeral. She had planned everything for a discreet burial service in

Pirenópolis. When I got back, I arranged to have a mass said for her in the Carmo Church, beside the cemetery. The church was empty except for the last three rows, completely filled by a group of children accompanied by four nuns. Only then did I learn that Guilhermina supported the city's orphanage. I spent the afternoon after the mass immersed in the waterfall. The caretakers, sitting on the grass nearby, told me that Guilhermina had died painlessly, almost smiling, a book open on her chest, the cats playing with a huge rag doll at her feet. And so I inherited the farm, the Night Stand, the cats, and the hatbox.

For me, the hatbox, with its gaps between letters and photographs, suggested more than it actually showed. By now Fernando and I were in considerable disagreement, he concentrating on the documentary side (which I considered important, but not essential), whereas I was open to fantasy, to everything that *didn't* show up in the hatbox. Because I believe Guilhermina, though she told me most of her story, mischievously concealed certain parts, giving some hints but withholding others. The untold parts remained suspended in her silences and sudden changes of tone or subject. She concealed, for instance, the whole Marie-France affair, in a rare moment of shyness. (Unlike Fernando, I believe this was due to the intensity of what she felt for Marie-France, and not because of simple prudery.) Probably she concealed other moments, through lapses of memory or because she was absorbed with reliving events and sensations. And she told me some things I chose not to share with anyone.

In short, Guilhermina had earned the right to preserve a few mysteries. And she defended that right at a very deep level. She could, for example, fall suddenly silent thinking about a glass of white wine, taken alone on some terrace over the Seine at sunset, and not elaborate on that instant of pleasure. Or she could speak about a particular scene in a tone that would cause me to keep it to myself. Since her life had been framed by two periods of almost absolute seclusion (in her first youth, during her seven years of marriage to Maia Macedo, and in her old age, on the farm in Goiás), it was possible that the music of her personality, to borrow a metaphor dear to Fernando, was more in the pauses than in the notes. As a woman, I felt this distinctly. Although I never could get inside the skin of the *character,* I think I knew the *person* better, for the simple reason that I liked her immensely. And because I liked her, I'm trying hard to remember conversations among my parents, aunts, uncles, and grandparents, in the hope of retrieving some further fragment relating to her.

Because they did talk about her, when the family would get together in Leme for Sunday dinner at my parents' house. They talked about her because she was rich, or much richer than we were—we paid rent and didn't even have a car—and rich relatives are always fascinating. (From my corner of the table I imagined, for instance, that she must have had a TV.) They talked about her also because she had rebuffed all attempts at reconciliation made by my grandfather or others in his name. Finally—and this was very unusual when I was a child—they talked because she had traveled abroad alone, met people, smoked cigars (a snapshot of her smoking a cigar had come into my grandfather's hands, nobody knew how), and who knows, maybe even had *an adventure.* "Which would in no way make her an adventuress," as my grandmother always hastened to clarify every time this hypothesis was raised by some more daring daughter-in-law. (What a shame, I would think, since I always connected that word with "The Angel," a radio serial my older brother and I used to follow, inseparably fused with the trumpets of the "Esso Reporter" and news of the Korean War.)

But what I see most clearly in these Sunday dinners, when I try to remember something associated with Guilhermina, is a vague, accepting sadness in my grandfather's eyes. I watch the sadness slowly take over his face each time the conversation arches itself widely over other themes ranging from the water shortage to the cook's meat patties, from our next-door neighbor's love affairs to the suicide of President Getúlio Vargas, and lands for refueling on Guilhermina. It is a subject my grandfather never brings up, but on the other hand never avoids. He contributes a word here or there, like a spectator who maintains the hope that the conversation, exactly like in the radio serials, will next time hold the words, "Know what? Guilhermina's in town, I met her walking down the street the other day, and . . ."

That's why I think it's beautiful, so many years after my grandfather's death, that I was the one to find Aunt Guilhermina and to perceive that, in her own way, she also had lived a radio serial. Except that hers progressed backward in time. She only felt able to open herself to her brother after his death. Something similar happened between her and the Honorable Maia Macedo: she told me that, at bottom, she only opened herself to him *before his death*. Not when he was alive, and not after his death, but in that precise interval in the wine cellar *before his death*.

Chapter Thirteen

Guilhermina hardly drank. However, on one of my visits to her farm we opened some wine I had brought from Rio, to go with a pâté the caretaker's wife had made under her instruction. I think that wine literally loosened her tongue. Sitting in her rocking chair on the porch, she suddenly smacked her lips, praised the wine, and, after another sip, said that good wine should be kept in a wine cellar. I made some light comment about how difficult it was to have a wine cellar in a Rio apartment. She laughed softly in the half-light and patted one of her cats on the head. Then she remarked,

"You know, I used to have a wine cellar once."

She might have said, "I like to eat corn on the cob" or "Please hand me that ball of wool." After another pause and another sip, she proceeded, her head leaning against the back of the chair and her eyes on the sky, where a flight of steps suddenly appeared between the stars:

"When I started down the steps with him, the whole staircase smelled like wine; Joaquim had broken two bottles when he emptied the wine cellar out that afternoon."

"Joaquim?"

"The manservant in the plantation house."

89

That was how she finally let me enter her story, like someone opening a trapdoor hidden behind a tapestry.

"Four years before we had gone down that same staircase together, he with firm steps, a silver candelabra in one hand. Now it was I who went down in front of him, and he would set one foot down, then the other, slowly, his hand on my shoulder so as not to fall, and I aided him with the politeness of the hangman who helps the condemned criminal to climb up on the scaffold. We went down and down . . . the steps seemed endless, there was always one more . . ."

. . . on the path down to hell. On that first occasion four years before, the Honorable had described to her a moment of magic, a long scene sprinkled with perfumes and foam. Now, on the second trip down, the cat still meowing behind the door, he descended between his wife and the Baroness—because on the veranda he had just been dreaming about Maria Stella, a dream he had often had, one that had also taken place in a remote cellar.

"I went into the barred area with him. He stayed near the bars and I walked over to the far wall, gluing my back to the stones. The cold made me think of that bloody, freezing sheet of seven years before, which was good; it helped me. So we stayed there together, in a space fifteen feet square, with the bars half-open. I spoke very little, the minimum necessary, and showed him the shelves that were to be removed so the spare parts for his machines could be stored there. He was tired, impatient, and inattentive, probably hungry, and wanted to go back up. He looked like an old circus bear, half-dizzy in an unfamiliar place."

Another sip of wine.

"So I moved past him slowly, in about three steps, as if the matter were settled. He took a last look around him and also turned as if to go. I slammed the bars shut a hand's breadth from his face. Clang! He looked at my fingers that were quickly locking the pad-lock, made a vague gesture, and asked, laughing foolishly, "What's this, Guilhermina?"

―――

There was no sadness, relief, or joy in her voice. Just the concentration of one trying to establish a fact with precision.

"I don't know what came over me. I was tenser and stiffer than a bamboo rod. I started to laugh too. Then I think I let out a shriek, raising my arms up: *"WHAT'S THIS? THIS?!"* and we both gave incredible peals of laughter, on opposite sides of the bars. We laughed like banshees for a long time. Then suddenly he lunged for me."

Guilhermina brings her hands up to her throat and head.

"That's when he must have pulled out some strands of my hair."

I remain silent in my hammock during the pause that follows. Guilhermina refills our glasses.

"I told you that he died of hunger in the cellar, didn't I? He was stronger than I imagined; he lasted five nights and four days. At the end he sang pieces of opera. I had no idea he liked opera. Actually, I knew so much about that man, and at the same time so little. Yes, he sang opera. But it sounded like a damaged record, played at the wrong speed. . . ."

. . . *like Hal in 2001,* I want to say, confusing my eras and realizing just in time that the comparison calls for a 78 rpm record, the nasal voice broken by scratches coming from the little speakers, like on a radio program my parents used to listen to religiously when I was little, which featured poetry read to a background of tango music: *"Es tarrrde, amor, debo partirrr."* But the old lady facing me, her dark blouse and white handkerchief suddenly coming into sharp focus, is describing other sounds.

"He shouted and appealed, he ran the gamut from tenderness to indignation, but I couldn't hear a word. I slumped onto the nightstand and tried to get my breath back, ignoring him behind the bars. Finally he stopped talking, his eyes resting heavily on me. I felt awkward in the sudden quiet. With a quick motion I turned off the light. He murmured again, very softly, in the darkness, "But

Guilhermina! I'm hungry, Guilhermina . . . what about my dinner?"

Where was my grandfather in 1933, when that happened? If Guilhermina was twenty-one, he must have been twenty-five or twenty-six. He was already a practicing lawyer, graduated from the Rio de Janeiro Law School and engaged to marry my grandmother. He had a small second-floor office on Carmo Street, which he maintained throughout his life and which I even visited as a child. Where was the octogenarian Maria Stella di San Rufo during Holy Week of 1933? Hailing Mussolini from the windows of her castle?

"We stayed silent in the dark for a long time. Little by little I calmed myself and so did he. It was better that way, as he quickly understood. The old man really was intelligent! When I closed the door behind me and turned on the light to go up the stairway he screamed one last time: *'GUILHERMINA!'* "

But the door was solid and the door after it, many steps above, was lined with two layers of felt she had glued there a couple of years before.

"The cat was still there. I didn't hear another thing until I smashed a glass on the kitchen floor. I always was rather clumsy in the kitchen. Not outside the kitchen, mind you—I did beautiful crochet work, and was clever with my hands. As a child I used to fix my own dolls. Did you play with dolls as a child?"

"Yes, I guess so . . . yes, some."

"I played with dolls until I was fourteen. If I hadn't married, I think I would have played with them even longer. In my time, girls played with dolls until very late, sometimes to the age of fifteen or sixteen. The first time I met Carlos Augusto he gave me a doll."

A long pause and another gaze into the starry sky. The somber tones of the wine cellar give way to the brightness of a child's bedroom.

"I was in my room, and my parents came in with Carlos Augusto following them. He had to duck his head to get through the door, and he looked directly at me and smiled at my parents. I perceived immediately—children sense these things—that it was a smile of approval. Behind his back he held a doll and a small box wrapped in tissue paper. Everybody was laughing a lot, as if they were accomplices together in some practical joke. Except your grandfather, who tiptoed into the room behind the other three. I was dressed up in my best clothes. 'Today you're going to have an important visitor,' my mother had told me. And she herself had given me a bath, something she hadn't done for over two years. 'A mother's bath,' as she said. Did your mother ever give you *a mother's bath?*"

"Not that I remember."

"I thanked him very much for the doll and put the little box on the bed. The doll was made of cloth. Nevertheless it was the biggest and most luxurious one I had ever been given, all dressed in silks and laces. Beside the others it looked almost disproportional, and I felt my other dolls shrink a little on their shelves. I thought to myself, "*That man was very large, to hide such a big doll behind his back!*" Still I was growing more and more ill at ease, not understanding what was going on. Nobody said anything, everyone just kept smiling and laughing, but some clue was clearly missing. After a while my father (your great-grandfather was a tall thin man) bent slowly over the bed, picked up the little box, and placed it once again in my hands. There was something solemn and grave in that gesture. 'Open it, Guilhermina, open it,' he said with a tenderness that struck me as rather mournful. And so, to dispel the cloud that I sensed on the horizon, I made a little joke: I said I was prepared for one surprise, but not for two. Then the three of them dissolved in laughter; it was an absurdly exaggerated gaiety, especially because your grandfather continued serious and completely mute in his corner. I stood on tiptoe and tried to look behind that man who seemed to occupy half the room and blocked my view of the door, thinking that with all this merriment there must be something outside in the hall, maybe a puppy or a kitten. Mama said, 'It's not out there, it's in here, silly!' Then the visitor patted me on the head and said my name: 'Guilhermina.' The tone was solemn and made me grow alert: it seemed as if he were about to make a speech. But he closed his mouth and didn't say anything more. There was an uncomfortable pause. To do something, I opened the little box, carefully so as to reuse the tissue paper, as I had been taught at school. From the corner of my eye I could see your grandfather take two steps toward us. Inside the box was a ring. I had never had a real ring, except for a small gold-plated one from my first communion, and I was delighted. I let out a cry of joy and exclaimed, 'Mama, Papa, a ring! Look, Mama, how beautiful!' and showed it to them. 'It's a special kind of ring,' my father told me, in the tone you use to teach a child the difference between a rock and a planet. I put it on my finger right away, but it was much too large. I remember saying to my parents, 'It almost fits on my pinky and on my ring finger together.' From the way they looked at me, I could tell this wasn't quite the reaction they had expected. Then there was an extremely awkward silence. Papa coughed a bit. When he finally began to speak, I didn't hear another thing, I was taken by a strange sensation . . . his words, after the 'My daughter . . .' seemed made of rubber, bigger than the room itself, as if there were some kind of echo all around us. That man, the echo said, had come to ask for my hand in marriage. I didn't even try to laugh, because your grandfather was still completely serious and very pale, lost in a fog, and also because a sort of numbness was starting to paralyze my whole body. I believe that at that exact moment, before he disappeared from my life, your grandfather saw the future. My father kept talking to me as I stared down at the rug, and your grandfather, his arms hanging down and fists clenched, kept fading farther and farther away, receding into a mist. . . ."

I am back in Rio, eating Sunday dinner with my family, and I see again my grandfather's sad face lost in the fog.

"When the last thread of that echo that was announcing my fate gave way to a new silence, Mama took a little lace handkerchief from her pocket and wiped her eyes quickly, sniffling, 'My little

girl . . .' I shook my head no, slowly at first, then faster, I shook my head no for a month. I couldn't eat and I cried all the time, hiding in corners. There was nobody to cry with, because my parents, initially affectionate and understanding, quickly began to lose their patience; the question was settled. My mother actually did cry with me in secret, but her tears were more for herself than for me. She and my father were basically in agreement as to what was, in fact, a great project. Your grandfather, poor thing, started avoiding me as if I were a leper; I think he saw my attitude as one of betrayal and thus resolved the matter in his own mind. He had just turned seventeen and had managed to get our parents' consent to move to Rio and live with some cousins so he could start college. Your grandfather in college and I in space . . . On the other hand, my dear, what space it was . . . what space . . . Here's to you, Andrea!"

"Here's to you, Aunt!"

Chapter Fourteen

Escape, run away, flee, no question of that, right?"

"Only if I were to take the clothes on my back and nothing more, disappear into the woods, and end my days in some brothel—or, more probably, be brought home a few hours later, soaked and humiliated, in some neighbor's wagon, my dress all muddy. Andrea, my dear, think! It was 1926, the interior of the state of Rio. Imagine a family of decent but modest resources suddenly being promised lands, along with the honor of a powerful surname bestowed on their daughter. The difference in our ages was outrageous, but such things were quite common in those days. No, the question I asked myself for years had nothing to do with escape. I never even dreamed of running away. The question was: Why didn't I give in? Why didn't I make the best of it?"

"Like any other woman of your generation . . ."

"Of course. So much simpler . . . And to discover, with the passing of time, that Carlos Augusto, from the heights of his old age, was as innocent as I, a tender girl. So if it wasn't a story of victims and culprits, why keep my old hatred intact, why make it into a project? Why take revenge on one project with another? The answer I'm obliged to accept, no matter how many times I go back to the subject, is simple: little by little, I started to relish the idea of killing the old man. I mean, as I developed, read, meditated, and perceived the futility or relative injustice of the whole affair, the idea of his death became less and less vengeful in purpose. It took on another meaning, as if it were a diabolical mission in which I had suddenly become involved by some caprice of perverse gods. And the more I thought of myself as a cruel, cold murderess, the more pleasure I felt. Terrible, isn't it? You must be shocked by my stories."

"The other day when we were talking about the question of coldness and cruelty, you said something about your theory of levels, something to the effect that you had actually asked him . . ."

"I know, in the wine cellar, at the end. I was searching for some sort of absolution. He was almost dead, and I needed to be absolved, not of his death, but of the pleasure it gave me; I needed a way to manage my perversion. But let me explain more clearly. If we could perhaps move to another period and look at this from a different angle. Take my arrival in Paris, for instance. When I arrived, the whole Gervoise-Boileau clan was there, armed with a pince-nez to inspect me from head to toe. But do you think I let myself be intimidated? They were eating out of my hand after one smile in the foyer of their *hôtel particulier*. And when, on the afternoon of my first day there, I realized one of the boys had climbed up on a wardrobe in my bedroom and was watching me take a bath through a tiny, steamy window over the door, I felt like I was back in the wine cellar. Except that now the wine cellar was an ornate room with a marble bathtub under a high ceiling, surrounded by Marie Antoinette, her ladies-in-waiting, and her lambs framed by walls covered in dark green. After the endless train trip from Marseille, that bath was a blessing, the huge bathtub brimming with hot water, the aromatic salts and vapors relaxing my every muscle. Then suddenly, down in the corner of a mirror in front of me, I saw the face of the boy perched atop the wardrobe. He never knew I saw him. It was Patrick, the youngest of my cousins. Andrea, have

---

you ever felt pleasure at knowing yourself observed when you were completely naked?"

"Well, I once experienced something similar. . . ."

"Really?"

"And it was in a bathtub, too."

"What a coincidence!"

"In a film. Once I was part of a movie cast."

"But that's different. Completely different. Whoever observed you knew that you felt observed. Even the look in their eyes was probably discreet, their thoughts almost suspended. At least that's what I imagine; that's how I would feel in a similar situation. But not in my case. I controlled his intruding eyes like a magnet— and through them, the poor boy himself. I had only made love with one man up to then, and our relationship had been real on one level and completely false on all others. It was an intense relationship, as I said, but one which fulfilled a perverse function. And now something perverse was happening too, only much sweeter. It was as strong as the act of love itself. There behind me was a boy much younger than I, with a fragile, virginal appearance, his face contorted and breathless, probably experiencing a sublime moment. Patrick must have been about thirteen. I stayed in the water for an hour, taking care to raise myself up from time to time, rubbing my back languidly with the sponge, letting my arms hang over the sides of the tub, humming a little tune—until I stood up, always with my back to him, as excited as he was up on the wardrobe. When, very slowly, I turned in his direction and bent over to get a towel from a little bench, I experienced something entirely new: at that precise moment, I became aware of my body. In the years that followed, I would have many occasions to confirm the impression my body made on other people. But that was when I realized it for the very first time. Without even looking at the boy, I could feel his gaze glued to my skin, as I slowly dried off directly under his little window, never concealing myself totally with the towel, and touched myself in a rather—well, a rather perverse way. One knows how to do those things when one chooses, right?"

"Yes . . . yes, I guess so."

"Well. Cheers! It's so good to see the amusing side of these things, isn't it? I only shared this experience with one other friend, and we laughed about it too, but that was years and years ago. . . . The truth is this: the purest poetry isn't worth as much as one soft, sweet perversion. Oh . . . how many marvels men simply miss, without even realizing it . . . always in such a damn hurry, always unaware of subtleties. . . . But listen: that night at dinner, Patrick never stopped whispering into the ear of his older brother, Jean-Marc, who grew paler with every word. At eighteen, Jean-Marc was tall, with disheveled hair, and went about in somber-colored clothes, looking like he had escaped from a poem by Victor Hugo. The conversation was going like a house afire among the adults; we were eating pheasant and talking of a Brazil that I reinvented with each new sentence, but my attention remained fixed on those two brothers who ogled me incessantly between whispers. Their mother, at one point, laughed and said, " *'Mais vous semblez avoir un succès fou, ma chère cousine. . . .'* ('You're really quite a success, my dear cousin. . . .') Once again I felt naked and this time the delight was even greater, since I was dressed and the table crowded. That same night Jean-Marc walked straight across the huge salon, bowed to me, clicking his heels together, and invited me to go for a walk in the Bois de Boulogne. I smiled and refused. What was the hurry? And why the heel clicking, if he looked like a poet? I opted to play cards with the little sister, Anne-Marie, a gentle and even lucid form of perversion, for I had already made up my mind how this story would end. And indeed, after trailing me for three days and nights on end, Jean-Marc couldn't stand it anymore. He came into my room in the middle of the night and went directly to my bed, sobbing and trembling, as if he had had a nightmare and was look-ing for comfort between my sheets. *'Laisse-moi faire, laisse-moi faire,'* he begged, let me do it, let me do it, and of course I did. His body was very much like mine, as fragile and as white. Although he was very tall, he was so light he seemed to float. We floated together through the night, fell out of bed twice, and the next morning I was head over heels in love. Have you fallen in love many times in your life, Andrea?"

"Fallen in love, fallen in love . . ."

"Yes, when you think the world has stopped, when your breath feels short, when every drop of blood in your body rushes to your face, when your legs give way under your own weight, things like that. . . ."

"No, not many times. And the way you describe, with that intensity, not for ages."

"But you know what it's like. Well, I didn't. For me, the world really did stop for two weeks. I laughed, I told stories, I charmed people, I radiated energy; I went back to acting and feeling like a child. But two weeks after my surrender to Jean-Marc, there appeared in my relatives' home a blond-haired man a little older than I. During dinner, he inclined his head over my shoulder and asked softly, *'Aimez-vous les ballons, mademoiselle?'* "

"The Danish guy?"

"I felt terrible. I didn't have the courage to look at him or at Jean-Marc either. I felt like a traitor, without ever betraying anyone. Was this love, then? Of course, Jean-Marc didn't notice anything. If he had, he would have gone crazy. One millimeter away from the abyss, he was absolutely secure in our love. And I really did love Jean-Marc, the way a person loves light after darkness."

"Then . . . why . . . ?"

"Why let it happen? Out of fear. And perversion. Peter was a distant relative of the Gervoise-Boileau family, Danish and an amateur balloon champion. With him, the only danger was falling from his balloon. With Jean-Marc, I had lost control, body and soul. The following afternoon Peter took me up in his balloon and . . ."

"Auntie, I don't believe you!"

"Yes, dear, in the little basket under the balloon, flying over Fontainebleau . . . and he never took off his cap, a little red-and-white felt one; it was so funny, that little cap of his. . . ."

Chapter Fifteen

———

During those first months I spent in Paris I started to live my real life. Everything was new to me. You understand, once I had made up my mind to kill Carlos Augusto, I didn't think for one second about myself or what could happen to me. It was sort of as if *nothing else* could ever happen to me, good or bad. I never thought about being caught or not being caught, about being tried or going to prison. I didn't even worry about those things. For seven long years I made my plans thinking always about him and never about myself. Even if I had been caught with him dead in the wine cellar, it would have been worth the effort. Definitely. My goal was not to survive and, still less, to profit. That's why I acted with such assurance and tranquillity. Perhaps that's why I managed to bring the whole thing off so successfully."

"Then the unexpected occurred. Or rather, something occurred that I hadn't sought in any conscious way: the precautions I took to move the plan forward proved so perfect that they placed me above suspicion. And along with my impunity, I gained an additional bonus, that of wealth. So much the better: I was free, rich, and could do whatever pleased me with my life. Like a slave who suddenly finds himself unexpectedly free, I lived in my golden

———

hideout, my eyes open to good and bad, my mind open to heroes and villains—as long as they were minimally interesting. No prejudices and plenty of money. Ready for life. Free of guilt or fear. Having read a few books. And having killed a man through the gods' carelessness—lesser gods, because I felt my story had everything in it except grandeur. I wasn't Joan of Arc, or Antigone, or one of the heroines of my childhood books. The fairy princess who, at age fourteen, had been presented a doll by her old bridegroom, had given way to a witch addicted to lovers and *marrons glacés*. A wealthy, attractive witch, vacationing in Europe, with X-ray eyes and a heart like a dry sponge."

"Take Peter, for example, the Danish balloonist. He appreciated my body, but loved my money. This understood, he was actually an interesting man, on a fine line between elegance and seediness. Even as his balloon descended from the heavens on our first trip, he was already whispering into my ear some detail about a project of his, always postponed, of buying a new balloon. Through an indiscretion (perhaps calculated) on the part of my cousin and host, he had learned of two monetary transfers to London in my favor. These tidy sums had moved his observant soul, an aristocratic soul housed in a handsome body, an unbeatable combination if it weren't for his poverty. For Peter, poor thing, was indeed a pauper by the standards of that clan; he could hardly maintain his old balloon or pay the rent for his lodgings in a discreet Saint-Cloud hotel. In a wretched estate settlement that causes such trauma in families of a certain class, his older brother had inherited the ancestral lands, his sister had received a dowry for her marriage, and he had ended up with some of the silverware, which he soon sold. Thus his passion for clouds and his gaze forever turned toward the skies."

"These things are mysterious by definition, but what most attracted me to him—a perverse factor, mind you—was to sense his excitement when he learned about my money. My money only interested me marginally. But it became a source of excitement for both of us. He was like a greedy child in a room full of golden chocolate coins, hardly able to keep himself from grabbing them all at once and stuffing them into his mouth. For me, it was like an aphrodisiac, to feel my body framed, ornamented, by the power of my money, as if through an error in projection I was slightly out of focus. It was an indescribable sensation, his hand, out of sync with his heart, stroking my skin. It was delicious, Andrea, like a new perfume, the musky kind that you only use occasionally because it's so strong. . . ."

"And what about Jean-Marc?"

"Tireless in bed, every night. The nights were his. Jean-Marc with his body like a feather and his enormous heart beating against mine, Jean-Marc with his inflamed discourses and poetry, his vows of love and his attacks of jealousy—jealousy of the future, because to him, poor boy, the present was wound up in our sheets and therefore secure. At the breakfast table, his parents would look at us with worry. A languor surrounded us both, punctuated by unmet glances and half-murmured sentences. Poetically depraved by night, by day we were two vestal virgins with circles under our eyes."

"Patrick, all this time, continued his contortions on top of the wardrobe like the snake of a demented fakir, for I maintained for him the ritual of drying myself slowly beneath his steamy window. Sometimes I would come back from afternoons spent in Peter's arms and bathe in preparation for the nocturnal embrace of Jean-Marc. Patrick was the andante between the allegros of my concertos. And like all good andantes, he furnished me with majestic and profound moments as I bathed in his eyes."

"Then, spring came. We went to Normandy, where the family had property, *une maison de campagne* as they described what, to me, looked more like an old castle. I went back to reading and riding horseback, and gathered mushrooms while my relatives hunted duck and rabbit. I didn't like hunting, I've always hated any kind of cruelty to animals, but I loved to ride horses, in a wild way.

My years on the plantation had made quite an Amazon out of me."

"Those were delightful days. It was my first contact with the countryside of France, which I was to know so well years later. The ancestors of the Gervoise-Boileau came from that region; the family had been established there for three or four centuries. I perceived very clearly a sense of ownership that went well beyond the possession of an old château, or the lands and forests around it. The animals they hunted belonged to them through almost divine right and, in that sense, were practically accessories in the hunt, creating at most small tactical difficulties by running or hiding, in order to give more flavor to the hunters' noble pleasure. My relatives laughed at me when I made comments to that effect, *'elle exagère, notre cousine,'* they would cry in chorus around the table. But at heart they adored it when I expressed things they knew to be true. Even the servants, themselves descendants of a long line of peasants and domestics who had faithfully served the Gervoise-Boileau through the centuries, mentally nodded their heads in agreement. If the walls of the château could have spoken, they too would have agreed."

"My cousins had only planned to stay in the country for a week. When they began to speak of going back, I asked to stay a little longer, alone with the servants, for I was quite enchanted with the place. Of course it was out of the question. *'Ça ne se fait pas, ma chère petite,'* my hostess replied anxiously. Then in a kindly impulse, Anne-Marie offered to stay with me, as she still had a few days of vacation left, and that somehow made things legitimate. In the attic room where we would meet furtively, Jean-Marc had three fits of rage, which I handled elegantly, and they all went off, leaving me in peace with Anne-Marie in the midst of that idyllic countryside."

"Anne-Marie was a timid, genteel girl of fifteen, tall and thin, but very graceful in her gestures and movements. She probably suspected what was happening between her brother and me, but she didn't pry or ask questions, since certain barriers must have seemed insurmountable to her young eyes. Her company was restful; it did me good. To this day I remember the hours we spent reading under the trees, our walks along the river Iton, our interminable dinners by candlelight upon an interminable table, just the two of us. The servants in uniform and the night breeze whispering against the windows. In spite of the difference in our ages, we were basically two girls, and we giggled about everything. After those two agitated weeks that had followed my arrival in Paris, I recovered with her, in that short lapse of time, the pleasure of an almost childlike friendship. We shared little complicities as girls will, and spent whole afternoons in the attic fixing old dolls."

"I talked about myself a lot to Anne-Marie, about my married life. To her it seemed monstrous that a girl of fourteen should have been given in marriage to a man well over sixty. In France, according to her, this only happened among the royal families or in a Molière play. I explained that in poorer countries the practice was far from unknown, and actually surprised myself by justifying somewhat the decision my parents had made on my behalf without my knowledge."

"This personal serenity, combined with the beauty of the landscape bursting into spring, helped me to reflect more clearly on my future. Since that time I've always thought a traveler should never enter an unknown country through the portals of its largest cities but rather through its villages and fields. It's so much more natural, easier, and people reveal themselves in such a different and more harmonious light . . . coherent in their words and actions. In no time at all the country becomes part of you."

"For the first time since my arrival, I began to consider seriously the possibility of staying in Europe for a few more months, largely due to that peaceful countryside with its hills, fields, thickets, and winding river that appeared and disappeared as it followed the planes of the landscape unfolding before our eyes. Nothing tied me to Brazil, except memories I preferred to leave behind. And since, in reality, nothing tied me to anyone or any particular place, those days spent with Anne-Marie, recalling my childhood among the colors of Cézanne and van Gogh, consolidated a sensation of independence that stayed with me throughout my life. At the same time, the idea of abandoning Jean-Marc and Peter was developing little by little in my mind. Both of them suddenly seemed to me crude and unfinished, like two noisy, greedy children. The sum of the two reduced each one to very little."

"Beside me, Anne-Marie, reading the countess of Ségur and pulling the petals off daisies, addressed me as *vous*. I wasn't even ten years older than she was, but I had been married and was a widow. It was very hard for her to say *tu*. For that very reason she merits a special place in my memory, such was the seductive power of that syllable, that *vous*. It was a disturbing thing. *'Cousine, voulez-vous vous baigner avec moi dans la rivière cet après-midi? Dites oui, cousine, je vous en prie, dites oui. . . .'* ('Cousin, would you like to swim with me in the river this afternoon? Say yes, Cousin, I beg of you. . . .') Do you speak French, Andrea? You must study French, my dear. I cannot imagine a language more beautiful or more subtle. The delicacy of that *vous* was a source of enchantment and mystery to me. Her parents, Carlos Augusto's cousins, always addressed each other as *vous* in the presence of others, even intimate friends. *'Mais ma chère, ne croyez vous pas que . . .'* I found that formality so unusual for a relatively young couple who, according to Jean-Marc, still permitted themselves the intimacy of sleeping in the same bed. *'Ils se disent tu dans les nuits de grand amour,'* Jean-Marc assured me, *'mais ils n'ont jamais passé une nuit blanche'* ('They call each other *tu* on passionate nights . . . but they have never made love all night long'), he swore as the first light of dawn appeared, leaving under my pillow an essay on Radiguet."

"Anne-Marie was at the age for confidences. She attended a Catholic school and was a good student, but already she felt her destiny tied to the will of others, discerning a probable marriage lurking around some corner. I recommended that she read certain books and try to distance herself from predetermined routes, and that she gain about five pounds. I did for her what Flávio Eduardo, almost without meaning to, had done for me a few years before. I don't know if it had results; I lost touch with her when I left her family and proceeded on my journey. I hope I was of some help, for she was a tender and sensitive creature. '*Chère cousine, voulez-vous que je vous lise quelques pages de Delly?*' ('Dear Cousin, should I read you a few pages of Delly?') What, I wonder, happened to Anne-Marie? Could she still be alive somewhere in Europe? Could she still be reading Delly? Today she would be over sixty . . . Carlos Augusto often wondered what had become of the people in his past. The same thing is happening to me today. I'd like to write a book that someday, rather by chance, would fall into the hands of my remote acquaintances. On some part of the planet, a friend suddenly raises his eyes from the page and cries to a deaf maidservant, '*Tiens . . . mais c'est moi, ça. . . . C'est de moi que parle cette vieille folle.*' ('Hey, but that's me. . . . It's me that old fool is speaking of!')."

"As the days went by, however, I started to feel oppressed by the sweetness of the young cousin with whom I now shared a bedroom and who confided to me her small youthful anxieties. Also, when I thought of Paris and those two men awaiting me with their demands and expectations, running on their stupid parallel tracks, I felt a little as if I were suffocating. This sensation, combined with the independence I was beginning to cultivate, made me realize I had to leave, escape, travel alone again somewhere, anywhere. I was saved by Carlos Augusto, my old ghost, and the sunny Italy of his memories: when I opened a bottle of liqueur for Anne-Marie one very rainy night, the almonds of his youth assaulted my nostrils. The next day I merrily packed my bags and we went back to Paris. Anne-Marie seemed surprised and a bit disappointed, but she agreed."

"Back at my cousins' house, I wrote two letters of farewell to my suitors, in which I lied about the duration of my absence, took a last bath in the big tub for Patrick (whom I unmasked with a little scream), said good-bye to my cousins, and took the train to Italy.

Jean-Marc thought that I was traveling the following day, and was at the lycée when I actually left. His parents, on the other hand, realized the misunderstanding was on purpose and foresaw that I wouldn't return. They could barely conceal their relief; Jean-Marc's studies were going dreadfully, a circumstance which, lacking another explanation, they attributed to me."

"As for Peter, he literally disappeared behind the clouds in his new balloon and I never heard of him again . . . the longings derived from simple pleasures are generally light ones. Passion complicates things so much, don't you think? How it complicates! Jean-Marc, poor thing, died in the war shortly after that. They say he tried to take a tank armed only with a bayonet. Ah, men, always swinging back and forth between their tanks and their pianos, their bayonets and their balloons. . . ."

Chapter Sixteen

A few days before our trip to Normandy, Anne-Marie and I had met a pianist at a concert at the Salle Gaveau. He was sitting a few rows back from us, and in the first interval of the concert, he sent me a box of bonbons with a little note inside, full of incomprehensible gallantries. During the second interval, he offered Anne-Marie a hot chocolate and me a glass of champagne. His name was Paul Nat. He spoke in a confused, bubbling way, mixing seductive images with music and poetry. When we left, however, he lost us. It was raining hard, we were both running to get a taxi. I caught a glimpse of his distressed face searching for me in the crowd. Anne-Marie laughed hard and squeezed my arm. *'Cousine, il voux cherche, ne vous cachez pas, cousine . . . Un si gentil garçon . . .'* ('Cousin, he is looking for you, don't hide Cousin . . . Such a charming man')."

"I was only to see Paul Nat again three years later, in Montparnasse, completely by chance. It was during my final year in Europe. I didn't recognize him, but to judge by the way he greeted me, he hadn't played a single note on his piano without thinking of me in that three-year interval."

"Paul dressed with studied casualness, and his wild hair reminded me of Jean-Marc. He was in his late twenties, and believed in many causes. He wanted to be a composer, a politician, a thinker. When he made puns, or exaggerated his emotions slightly, he always gave me the impression that he was testing new ideas from a permanently effervescent collection. For that reason, he could be extremely tiring in spite of his charm. I had some difficulty accompanying him on these inner journeys and often yawned during his monologues, which intrigued him. It's hard to explain, but compared to me and what I had lived through, he seemed fragile, and his agitations almost pointless."

"Even so, I believe Paul was the best thing that happened to me during my years in Europe. In his company I met interesting people, musicians and writers, architects, filmmakers, journalists. His friends weren't exactly famous or successful, but they were in touch with well-known people. One had edited two films of Marcel Carné, another had been an apprentice in Lalique's studio and was currently working with Erté; a third wrote for *Le Figaro*. A fourth was to become, later on, assistant to Le Corbusier. We haunted the cafés into the wee hours, discussing politics and literature, and ambled through the streets of Paris when the city was asleep. We would travel in a group together to the south of France, and even rented a big house together one summer in Nice."

"When Paul and I met again, however, I was already another woman, very different from the girl who had just arrived in Paris and gone to the Salle Gaveau. Many things had happened to me and to those close to me; I now had the experience of two years in Italy and my trips to Istanbul and Agadir, and was more open to the world, though at the same time more protective of my feelings. Besides, the world was changing terribly all around us; the war was about to start . . . that complicated things a little, too. The landscape was gray and already smelled of gunpowder. The re-encounter with Paul, for that reason, had a flavor of farewell tinged with guilt. Many of our friends were to die in the war shortly thereafter."

"By then I was coming to grips with problems of another type. A good part of my money had already been used up; Flávio

Eduardo wasn't answering my letters, or was sending smaller sums each time. According to him the plantation was doing poorly; coffee prices in Europe were falling with the approaching war, and the lawyers and businessmen he consulted advised me to sell the property. But I didn't want to sell it, at least not just yet. I had planted more than coffee on that land. . . ."

"I started selling off my jewels, not that I had that many, and later I discreetly sold some clothes. My new friends always made fun of those clothes, anyway. They were a little like beatniks, my friends, before the term came into fashion. Take Paul: I met his father once, and then I understood him better. The father was just the opposite of the son, he seemed like one of those dignified figures in top hats in the background of a Renoir painting, watching a horse race through their binoculars."

" '*Mais travaille, ma fille,*' ('So work, dear girl,') Paul would say to me, irritated when I became worried over my diminishing funds. He encouraged me to paint or do ceramics or translate Brazilian authors into French. I actually tried, beginning with *Dom Casmurro,* but Andrea, I had never worked before and I hadn't been even remotely bothered by the fact. I considered that what I had accomplished between the ages of fourteen and twenty-one justified an existence without links or obligations of any sort to people, cities, or jobs. I felt as if I had discharged all duty to men and their rituals."

"Furthermore, I didn't consider myself an especially creative person, or at least I didn't worry about being one. I admired the energy of the people around me, but I didn't envy them. What had happened to me at fourteen had cut off something inside me, had rendered me sterile. You know, Andrea, I couldn't even have children. Not that I missed them much . . . well, such things are hard to judge. In the beginning with Carlos Augusto and later on in Paris, I did take a few precautions, but as nothing happened, little by little I paid less attention to the matter. Would you like to have children someday?"

"Yes, someday."

"I only thought about it seriously, and wanted to, when I married Joaquim Guilherme—for his sake more than mine. Well, I don't know. Where was I?"

"The question of work."

"Oh, yes, work. Paul, perhaps rightly so, thought my attitude was strange, and demanded that I take some action. Then we would fight and I would disappear for a few weeks to Sologne, where a girlfriend of mine had a cabin in the woods. He would get desperate, write a thousand crazy letters which I wouldn't answer. In fact, with Paul, everything was breakups, re-encounters, sudden crises of jealousy, surprises, misunderstandings . . . it was more my fault than his, really."

"This friend who had a cabin in Sologne was also important in my life. In a way, I could actually say I worked with her. She was important, among other reasons, because she made me laugh. She was a very strong, secure woman, much more experienced than I was. And older; she was in her thirties. She represented a contrast to my first months in Paris, a period marked by constant amorous duplicity culminating in my flight to Italy after I smelled the aroma from that bottle of almond liqueur. I actually met Marie-France on that very journey, on the train. She conveyed to me an immediate impression of solidity and resolution; I could feel she was a complete human being. Do you know what I mean?"

"Yes . . ."

"Do you really? Funny . . . certain phases of my life sometimes seem as if they were compressed, everything happened so fast and so very early . . . Oh well . . . I've forgotten where I was again."

"Marie-France . . ."

"Yes, Marie-France. I was seated alone at a table, looking over the menu and choosing my dinner carefully, when my train stopped in Geneva. A woman boarded and came directly into the dining car. She was talking through the window with two other women outside on the platform. I was always rather methodical when I ordered in a restaurant, and thus didn't pay much attention to what was happening around me. Generally, women delegate the dialogue with waiters to their male companions—not me. Even when accompanied by a man, I didn't give up the right to make my own choices, ask my own questions. Up to this day. Imagine, if after killing a man, I would be intimidated by a waiter! The more impatient my male friends would get in restaurants, the more questions I asked."

"My meal finally selected, a glass of Bordeaux before me, I gave a satisfied smile when the train started up again. I heard the last chuckles of the three women who were saying good-bye behind me. They seemed happy. I myself felt happy, remembering the guilty pleasure with which, a few hours before, I had made my departure from the Gare de Lyon. I had been frightened that Jean-Marc would burst into the station at the last minute. And I smiled thinking of the letter I had put under his pillow: *Je reviendrai, je te le jure* (I will come back, I swear), I lied on a piece of paper I had wrinkled up and smudged to suggest sobs and anxiety."

"But what if, guessing the worst, he had come home early, read the note, and run to the station. I was still laughing to myself, opening my napkin on my lap, when a woman's face, smiling among the small waves of steam, appeared reflected on the surface of my consommé. It was as if her face had superimposed itself over that of Jean-Marc and her smile had met my own. The woman took off her glove, made a gesture toward the chair opposite mine, and asked, *'Vouz permettez?'*

"She still had a few snowflakes on the collar of her coat, which she removed and placed over the back of the chair. Sitting down, she looked directly at me, said, *'Qu'est-ce qu'il fait bon ici,'* ('How nice it is here,') and rubbed her hands together with energetic pleasure, adding, *'Je crève de faim.'* ('I'm starving.'). She smiled with wolf teeth at the waiter and ordered champagne. She seemed very satisfied with herself, as if she had just closed a good business deal or taught a well-deserved lesson to a boring husband. Then, exactly as I had done, she discussed with the maître in detail the composition of the dishes she selected, and the more limited the choices, the more specific her questions and the longer their discussion. Our choices coincided. I never asked myself precisely why she had sat down at my table, since there were so many others available at that hour; it seemed a simple and natural gesture. She said she was the owner of a restaurant in Paris, had just spent a few days in Geneva, and was traveling to Italy on business. We talked of trivial things; I told her a little about myself and we enjoyed the evening together. And then almost before we knew it, we were crossing borders. There's something so symbolic about border crossings, don't you think? Do you like to travel, Andrea?"

"I love to."

"Have you ever traveled much?"

"Well, not a lot."

"Oh, what a shame . . ."

Chapter Seventeen

My aunt's wanderings through Italy remain plunged to this day in the most impenetrable mystery. I remember asking her various questions about that phase of her life, but she always answered evasively. Now, of course, I understand why. I can just imagine the whirlwind of adventures she and Marie-France must have been part of during those years. Had she spent much time in Italy or had she zigzagged back and forth over various borders? From the hatbox we had learned of a trip to Istanbul and another to Agadir. Fernando wondered if she had helped to hire the green dwarfs. I went beyond that. On one of our afternoons at the farm, Guilhermina, without referring to the countries through which she was passing on the occasion, had mentioned a moment of panic at a border crossing, when her suitcases had been unexpectedly opened and searched by the police in meticulous detail. Nothing was found amiss. Then why tell me of the episode in half-terms, leaving an impression of alarm and anguish in the air? Had Marie-France, an obvious product of the Parisian *bas-fond*, taken advantage of Guilhermina's journey to Istanbul to order or to send something? Why had my aunt declared once, "I could actually say I worked with her"?

These were conjectures that I hadn't shared with Fernando,

fearing that he might be tempted to overemphasize (and quite un-
derstandably so) what actually fell within a hypothetical realm. But
the theme undeniably lent itself to certain interpretations, especially
in the light of those two years veiled in silence and omission. *Banquet offered by Edouard,* the notation in pencil stated on the margin
of a menu. Who was that person she had dined with in Istanbul?

From her Italian phase only one episode had been preserved.
It was one to which Guilhermina referred with a certain wealth of
detail: her meeting with the Baroness di San Rufo, the Maria Stella
of her husband's memories, during the party in commemoration of
her ninetieth birthday at the family's castle near Sardone. What a
store of memories Guilhermina had carried through the portals of
the ancient fief where her husband had lived out his unforgettable
adventure . . . What feelings she must have had, waiting along with
dozens of relatives, friends, and simple people of the region, for
Maria Stella to put her feet on the same enormous stone steps down
which she had glided toward Carlos Augusto nearly sixty years earlier. And the Baroness, after a long wait, had finally emerged from
the upper galleries of the castle and come down the steps, except
that, to Guilhermina's surprise, she was shrunken and withered,
and carried in the strong arms of a manservant.

But the situation hadn't been even remotely awkward or pa-
thetic. On the contrary, it had actually served to underline the
dignity with which the Baroness, waving her bony hand, had ac-
knowledged the applause of those present, who shouted enthusias-
tically, *"Viva la Baronessa! Auguri Baronessa!,"* opening a pathway
for her as she descended. Guilhermina had waited until after the
relatives and more intimate friends had paid their respects to offer,
with a little curtsy, her best wishes to the little old lady now seated
in a huge red velvet armchair at the back of the room.

"Sono Guilhermina, la cugina venuta dal Brasile," she had said
with a smile, adding more softly, *"la vedova di Carlos Augusto."* ("I
am Guilhermina, the cousin from Brazil, the widow of Carlos
Augusto."). As the tremulous, half-lost gaze of the Baroness seemed

to drift from one face to another, Guilhermina reminded her that she had sent a note some three weeks before from Florence, announcing her passage through the region, to which the Baroness had responded with an invitation to her brithday festivities.

Maria Stella heard, but still didn't understand. She didn't seem able to associate Carlos Augusto (of whom she may have had absolutely no recollection whatsoever) with a widow younger than her own granddaughters. She just said *"Brasile . . . ah, si . . . Brasile, ahch'io ho dei parenti li. . . . Che bello dev'essere il Brasile. . . ."* ("Brazil . . . oh yes . . . Brazil, I think I have some relatives there. . . . How beautiful Brazil must be . . .") She smiled thoughtfully and was already turning her attention toward another planet when she asked, as if in a sudden flash of memory, *"e gli sciavi, sono stati finalmente liberati?"* ("and the slaves, have they finally been freed?") and extended her hand to the next guest, leaving Guilhermina lost in a wave of longing that was not even her own.

What also had disoriented Guilhermina, contributing to increase her sensation of helplessness, had been the realization that during the lapse of time separating her visit from that of Carlos Augusto, the village of Sardone had become a small city, expanding almost to the walls of the castle (which perhaps for that reason didn't seem as imposing as the Honorable's reminiscences had suggested) and dislocating, in this process, the fields and vineyards to more distant areas. A restaurant now operated in the old dungeon, to which customers gained access by means of an elevator. Guilhermina ate a bite in the restaurant, almost empty at that hour (the whole town was celebrating the Baroness's birthday on the floors above), and looked over the installations with a careful eye, trying, with the help of an illustrative floor-plan hanging on the wall, to situate the approximate site of the pleasures experienced, half a century before, by her ex-husband between those same old walls.

"You know, Andrea, when he wasn't having nightmares, Carlos Augusto almost always dreamed about his Baroness. She was

a very strong presence in his life. He had dreamed of Maria Stella the very afternoon we went down to the wine cellar together.

"And he had told me about that dream, the lovely and graceful woman leading a dazzled young man down a labyrinth of staircases, their smothered laughter echoing in the shadows, to undress and contemplate him for a long time, way before she drew close and touched his body. He spoke of the way Maria Stella had finally caressed him, without the slightest inhibition, as if he were made of clay and she was there to breathe life into him. And he described to me the precise moment when she had removed her clothes with one motion and he, intimidated, had laid down on the stone floor, indifferent to the cold that pierced his back."

By visiting the castle in Sardone, Guilhermina had, in a certain way, paid homage to Carlos Augusto's last days, as though ending an important cycle. Indeed, upon her return from Europe, she had gone almost directly to visit her husband's grave, as a way of exorcising those moments experienced in Italy and ridding herself of the sensation of helplessness which had come over her in Salerno. Between the walls of the castle she had spent a few minutes with an old woman who had no recollection of the ravishing siren that had once come down the same staircase to sink ineradicable roots into the memory of a young foreigner. Only the slaves had survived the test of time, and they only remotely, like a fragment of papyrus which, exposed to the light, suddenly disintegrates into dust in an archaeologist's hands.

In the castle, Guilhermina had also inquired about Maria Stella's husband, Baron Raffaele Rinaldo di San Rufo. Among those present, the younger guests knew nothing about him, and the older ones had visibly evaded the subject, giving her awkward looks. But among some older servants who were talking animatedly on one side of the courtyard, Guilhermina learned that the Baron had been mysteriously murdered thirty years before, against the walls of the monastery across from the castle, after fighting with attackers who surprised him as he returned from a walk. His naked body, bearing obvious signs of torture, had been discovered in the first hours of the morning by two shepherds.

"So before I left the city, I visited the monastery and tried to talk with the monks about the episode, but none of them would deign to answer my questions. The old Baron, an inoffensive being and such a confessed accomplice to his beautiful wife's affairs, had paid for some personal sin with his life against those monastery walls. What sin it was, one was forbidden to ask even the walls themselves. On my way out, a wasted and visibly deranged monk had suddenly emerged from a shadow and danced around me on the sunny patio, flapping his moth-eaten habit and screeching: '*Raffaele Rinaldo di San Rufo, Raffaele Rinaldo di San Rufo, Raffaele Rinaldo di San Rufo . . .*' How old he was, that skeletal, toothless man in his threadbare habit, in the middle of a little cloud of dust! And how old the Baroness had grown, tiny in her silken shawl, carried downstairs by a brawny manservant! I left Sardone with that echo in my ears, *Raffaele Rinaldo di San Rufo, Raffaele Rinaldo di San Rufo. . . .* Oh, Andrea, how time passes. . . . And now I'm the one who's old. Do you think I'm very old, Andrea?"

"No, Aunt, of course not."

"Are you sure, Andrea?"

"Of course, Auntie! Of course I'm sure."

"Hmm . . . A liar, just like your grandfather."

"Why? Did he lie a lot?"

"Yes, to me he did. He lied as brothers always lie to their younger sisters, without causing any apparent damage to me or to anyone else and giving me the impression that lying was a legitimate way to protect yourself from parents or strangers. Of course, he taught me how to lie too. I lied to my dolls and my cats, and that helped me later on, when I was married to Carlos Augusto: he became a child in my hands, sort of like an enormous live doll, without much chance of defending himself. Later, of course, I don't quite know, I became lost in my forest of half-truths, looking

———

for the way out and mistrusting myself and others. Actually, I would have liked to come out of that enormous fog where I spent my adult life. I didn't have the courage. That's why, when Joaquim Guilherme died, I bought this land and moved here to Goiás, just like Greta Garbo and her 'I want to be alone.' You know, I once met Greta Garbo in Paris. . . ."

"Really? Greta Garbo?"

"At Fouquet's. She was at a table nearby, with several other women who all looked like models, and a group of loud Americans who smoked cigars and called incessantly for champagne. They were commemorating the Parisian opening of *Camille*. We exchanged a few words, and she playfully forbade me to see the film. 'It iz terrible,' she said laughing from her table, she had drunk a little and her eyes were bright . . . how her eyes shone! After that night, I never believed she was sad and reserved, as people said. Anyway, at Fouquet's, she laughed a lot and seemed quite happy; we toasted everyone at our respective tables. When she left, she even turned around and waved good-bye to us. The other day I saw her picture in the newspaper: so old, hiding behind huge dark glasses, her coat collar turned up around her neck. But that evening we were both eternal; the distance between our tables was short, we both had our champagne and our friends, and we weren't hiding from anyone. Life has its moments . . . she had hers, I had mine. Of course she had her secrets. Better that way. Just think how boring to know *everything* about Greta Garbo. So much better to imagine . . ."

"And you never saw her again?"

"We lived together for ten years here in Goiás. But please, you mustn't tell anyone!"

"Oh, Auntie! . . ."

"A liar, just like your grandfather."

Chapter Eighteen

So now, what to do with this text which, when all is said and done, doesn't even belong to me? Revise it again and give it to Fernando?

When I began writing about Guilhermina, I could sense that her story possessed a life of its own. I had noted this on the afternoons spent with her at the farm. It was as if an anonymous background figure, lost among dozens of others on a large canvas, had suddenly taken advantage of a lapse in the observer's attention to jump into the foreground and then, not content with his feat, had slipped through the edge of the frame and landed on the floor, claiming his place under the sun. That was the impression Guilhermina gave me once the barriers of silence, time, and space had finally been broken.

And to think that Fernando, at least in the beginning, had vacillated between the two stories, our more immediate one and Guilhermina's! I hadn't. First of all, because my past with Fernando in Los Angeles hadn't been that remarkable. I was married then and in spite of Murilo's provincialism I loved him, jealousy, bicycles, and all. Nothing more restful than living with a bicycle salesman. Second, because the brief romance I shared with Fernando, when it finally happened, almost floundered on the banks of the waterfall where it began. Guilhermina was demanding; the story of her life left no space for other events. Thus the aunt who indirectly brought Fernando and me together again after ten years distanced me from him as she filled every available inch of space in our relationship.

But I have no complaints on that score. All in all, I actually prefer to have Fernando simply as a friend. True, our re-encounter has roots in the past, but in other people's past. I believe he'll agree with me in time. People sometimes enter certain relationships out of curiosity, to confirm the taste of old sensations—nothing wrong in that. But to insist is dangerous; the past gets lost and nothing very worthwhile is established in the present. I don't mean to deliver great truths here; I'm just stating what I feel. If I learned anything from Guilhermina's joys and frustrations, it was to be aware of my feelings and express them clearly, at least to myself.

Still, Fernando's appearance on the scene was essential to make me look at Guilhermina from fresh angles, and see possibilities I had left unexplored. Perhaps without intending to, Fernando stimulated me to review my aunt's behavior in the first years of her marriage, when, for purely strategic motives, she had plunged herself into the day-to-day life of her Honorable in an almost abstract manner. Using her husband's sexual appetites as a conducting wire, she had managed to share entire portions of his past.

Reviewing Guilhermina's story for myself in this more open and unhindered way, I guessed much more than I actually knew. Probably Fernando was secretly counting on this. Except that he committed a small error in judgment, because I will say nothing about my conjectures. The imagined script will not be filmed, not even if entire scenes jump out from between the lines or spotlights try to illuminate old secrets. The lenses will see nothing, not opium nor white-slave traffic. I even feel a somewhat clandestine pleasure in preserving what isn't mine, in declaring out of bounds what probably never existed.

I've asked myself repeatedly if Fernando's motivation to

recreate Guilhermina's story was limited to his desire to make a film. For those who make movies, or want to make them and can't, movies are everything. At first, of course, he simply wanted to re-live our past in Los Angeles. But later, I think he began to enjoy playing a game with the characters, approaching the story as if it were a jigsaw puzzle, looking for the piece that would eventually reveal the whole picture. But, as Fernando should know, such pieces, when they exist, are often mixed in other puzzle boxes.

So now, when we get together and talk about the results of our project (not even one hundred pages between the two of us) I am forced to discard all hypotheses, and believe purely and simply in Fernando's fascination for magic, for chance, for the unexpected. Magic, represented by a bleeding young bride who dreams of lock-ing up her tormentor behind bars, and the next morning opens a door that leads her down a flight of steps to realize her dream. Chance, personified by a new face superimposed on another in the vapors of a consommé, to fill a moment of loneliness. The unex-pected, brought about by an old invitation left in a mailbox, that would have gone into the wastebasket if it weren't for the term *nightstand*.

Nightstands aside, Fernando always had a special fascination for the hallways, furniture, old family photos, and small objects of this story we unearthed. With my help, on one of our last after-noons at the farm, he even re-created the entire physical layout of the old plantation house, a task that seemed useless and intermina-ble to me. Perhaps he was only using his talent as a set designer, I don't know. At any rate, for hours on end, we shined our flashlights among the curves, staircases, and corridors of the past, looking for some forgotten link which had never materialized, no matter how I tried to bring to life the rooms and furnishings of the old stage-setting. Fernando had registered the paintings, the decorative objects, the curtains, and the dishes, but his greatest interest was concentrated on the wardrobes and dressers, as if, moved by the simple force of his curiosity, I could command some drawer to open . . . (a power which I had, of course, but didn't exercise due to an almost sublime caprice).

The conversation had fortunately changed course when, amid that insane (and in my view futile) effort to visualize all those old settings, we had finally arrived at Guilhermina's bedroom. Crossing its threshold, we had examined the books on the shelf, patted the bedspread on the narrow bed, opened the window that looked out onto endlessly changing landscapes. How exquisite those canvases must have been, with their echoes, colors, shapes, and odors that challenged time itself. *How was it possible to paint like that?* she had asked herself. And who were those people, in another painting, another time, and another part of the world, embracing on the sidewalk?

Part Three

Chapter Nineteen

Behind her silences and omis-
sions, Andrea almost certainly concealed things from me. Last year
when we first met again in the Night Stand, she spoke freely and
torrentially about her aunt. Little by little, though, the flow of her
revelations grew smaller, until it ran completely dry and she
stopped answering my questions. She finally gave me the text I
asked her to write, but it was more like a synopsis or summary of
other texts, as if she had edited a larger work and kept the final
version of it for herself. That's her privilege, of course, and it didn't
cause any ill feelings between us—we continue to be friends, although we've seen less of each other lately. But it's an attitude I
have trouble understanding. Especially since, from a certain point
onward, the less Andrea talked, the more her silence seemed to
conceal.

So how could one not understand my desire to continue
investigating the subject on my own? I couldn't bear to reduce
Guilhermina and her memories to one more postponed project.
Especially since certain addresses from the hatbox full of old letters
and papers had attracted my attention. I had copied some of them
into a little notebook that I kept together with my notes. I had
acted without apparent motive, like a reporter who writes down

details to better ground his story in reality. The streets had poetic names, evoking parts of movies, and made me think of Arletty, Jean Gabin, Michelle Morgan, Jean-Louis Barrault, all wearing their raincoats and berets, or striped T-shirts, Pierrot costumes, saying *salut patron, bonjour mon petit, merci ma belle.* . . .

It's true that as soon as Andrea's interest in our project began to wane and she showed signs of impatience, I started to look at these notations more closely, asking myself what fate had befallen those people, if they were alive or dead, and what lives they had led in the half century that separated us. I reviewed my Parisian addresses again, trying to imagine the streets through which Guilhermina had walked with her friends and acquaintances before the war. The streets and alleys stirred my imagination just like, years before, the tuft of red hair had inspired Dr. Flávio Eduardo to find out what had happened to his old friend. Except that, in my case, the Honorable did not figure as the protagonist. On the contrary, he diminished in stature and importance with each passing day, giving way to other figures and personages. Of course, there was nothing to prevent him from suddenly returning to the foreground, rattling his bars or singing his operatic aria in the wine cellar. With Guilhermina and her story, it was hard to foresee which new actors would take center stage, and which others waited in the wings.

But every story usually has two or three watersheds, like successive movements in a concerto. If my finding Andrea again represented one of them, and the hatbox with its treasures possibly a second, then my trip to Paris, by opening new horizons for Guilhermina and her cast of characters, certainly represented another such moment of convergence.

Thus when I was called to the dean's office to learn of the university's participation in the Brazil-France Project, I received with great joy but small astonishment the news that I had been chosen to participate in the trip to Paris, replacing a colleague who, at the last minute, had come down with hepatitis. At once I began to review Guilhermina's addresses and those from the films of my adolescence: *Rue de la Harpe, Quai Voltaire, Place Clichy, Boulevard du Crime, Rue Fontaine, Place Blanche* . . . And I was already asking myself whether I should tell Andrea about this new irony of fate when, still feeling the breezes on the *Quai des Brumes* around me, I heard the voice of the good dean, joking with the others present: "Our professor has already embarked! . . ." The herald of my departure was right; there is no better news than an unexpected journey.

But I didn't tell Andrea about it. She would try to dissuade me from walking down those streets, and this would create an awkward situation between us. I don't blame her, although I disagree. My views on this are simple: in spite of being a faithful guardian, Andrea doesn't have exclusive rights to her aunt's story. She has the power, which she exercised, to refuse to open certain doors or compartments to my scrutiny. But she can't stop me from looking in other places.

So when I went to dig out my passport and apply for a visa, and accidentally came across the old addresses put away in the same drawer, I interpreted the coincidence as an additional sign from Guilhermina to me. I hesitated no longer. Without making it my primary goal, I resolved to continue investigating her story in my free time in Paris. I promised myself to tell Andrea everything at the right time, and someday I certainly shall.

During my first two weeks in Paris, however, I actually forgot about the matter, I was so taken up with my work and with the city itself. I had never been to Paris. On my only trip to Europe years before, coming back from the United States, my student budget hadn't allowed me to get beyond Spain and England. My work at the Sorbonne, on the other hand, was exciting and presented me with several challenges, beginning with the language, which I speak badly. I was much absorbed. I spent all my time running around on the job, enchanted with the city, which was slowly becoming part of me as it replaced the images borrowed from the books and movies of my earlier years. Then one rainy afternoon, I found myself in the Closerie des Lilas, savoring the past among the ghosts of Hemingway, Fitzgerald, and Modigliani, and absentmindedly watching the people who hurried down the Boulevard Montparnasse in front of me. Suddenly I felt Guilhermina's presence. She was sitting right beside me reading a newspaper.

I know very well that sooner or later I'll lose my wits to some degree, like everybody else. This prospect doesn't alarm me at all; in fact, I find it rather attractive. I like the poetry that takes control of people when they get senile. But I would have preferred to put this inevitable moment off a little longer. I'd like to get married, have three children, do a film, be accepted into a respectable social club. So Guilhermina's presence at the next table didn't amuse me at all; it worried me.

Outside, the fog was growing thick. People were heading home faster. The woman at my right kept on reading her paper, her red hair less than a yard from my shoulders. I had the sensation she was actively observing me. With great effort I managed to resist the temptation to turn around. Instead, I picked up my change and went out without looking back.

In the days that followed, however, the sensation of that presence grew ever stronger. Guilhermina went everywhere with me, interfered in my choices at the *bistrots* (where she would make me order unnecessarily expensive or complicated dishes), marched me down unknown byways, got me lost in alleys and unexpected side routes, not to mention what she did at night, when she would materialize against the shadows of my walls, mixed with the red neon of the Cinzano sign that blinked from the top of the building opposite my hotel. Guilhermina was demanding I get busy. It didn't seem fair, in her view, that my poor colleague from the university should be suffering from hepatitis for nothing. Weak and easily dominated as I am, I ceded to her demands. And notebook in hand, I went back fifty years: I returned to the trail of her story.

Chapter Twenty

Andrea had only referred to the Gervoise-Boileau in very generic terms: a couple with three children, the eldest of whom had probably been a little in love with her aunt. With him, it seems, Guilhermina had had a brief affair. Andrea knew very little about the daughter (Guilhermina had played cards with her, and they went to the theater together every so often), and of the youngest nothing at all. But that Parisian branch of the Maia Macedo family had certainly played an important role in Guilhermina's initiation to Europe. Andrea's aunt would never have spent her first months in Paris in a banal or colorless atmosphere. To some extent, the scenery must have been in keeping with the character.

At least as far as physical grandeur went, it was. The Gervoise-Boileaus' *hôtel particulier* on Avenue George V, today remodeled and transformed into the Kuwaiti Embassy, was an elegant and imposing building. According to what the porter told me, the last time it had changed hands had been in the fifties. The remodeling and restoration was done in the early sixties; of that he was certain, since he had taken part in the work. But the construction of the building dated from the end of the nineteenth century. He had never heard of the Gervoise-Boileau family, nor had anyone in the neighborhood. *"Non, je regrette, non, je ne vois pas du tout. Essayez le bottin."* ("No, I'm sorry, no, I don't know them at all. Try the phone book.")

So I tramped through the city after clues that might lead me to the old family or its descendants. After much walking, lots of metro rides, several telephone calls, and a few mistaken encounters—by then Guilhermina was already showing obvious signs of impatience—I finally found a thread, but in Normandy, not Paris. Taking advantage of a sunny weekend, I boarded a train to Evreux and then a bus that brought me over secondary roads to a village called Gervoissy.

Patrick Gervoise-Boileau is visibly intrigued by my visit. *"Du Brésil, dites-vous?"* he had asked, shouting over the telephone (he's rather deaf) when, after talking with a great many of his relatives, I had finally found the right branch of the family. But though he's intrigued, he knows how to wait, a talent one only develops with age. I wait too, as we talk amenities and he tells me a little about Gervoissy and the region where we are. He explains that his family has lived in this part of the country for five centuries and is probably descended from Charles Berry, a brother of Louis XI, who was duke of Normandy for a few years during the fifteenth century. He refers to the religious wars that for generations had decimated Catholics and Huguenots. He adds that he himself had spent part of his childhood in a manor house in a valley near this very village. Didn't I perhaps notice the estate from the train window, he inquires.

He calls my attention to the very peculiar structural characteristics of the house, which he describes as typical of a certain style found nowhere else in France. Wood and large stones compose a type of architecture called *colombage,* the origins of which go back to the remotest invasions of the Vikings into Normandy. He mentions the Great Cross of Saint André that used to take up one whole wall of the second floor. He recalls with affection words whose sonority I register without understanding them: *torchis, bauge, til-*

lasse, a terminology that seems rooted like a tree in his language and his past. He offers, if I am interested, to arrange a visit to the property, explaining to me that the new owners are very amiable, but rarely spend much time in the region—they are foreigners. He remarks that, in any case, the caretakers are direct descendants of the servants who had helped him hunt rabbits when he was a boy, or to fish on the banks of the river Iton, where he and his brother and sister also loved to swim.

Little by little my companion—we drink a *kir* in a bar called A La Salamandre in the principal square of Gervoissy—seems reassured as to my intentions and even emits a few gestures of goodwill toward me. He offers me a cigarette, indicating to the waiter that the next round of drinks is on him. He's a sharp old man, rosy skinned, and carries a cane. In spite of the spring sunshine, he is wearing winter clothes: woolen pants, a suede jacket, a plaid flannel shirt, and a beret. He tells me that when he retired ten years ago, he couldn't resist buying a cottage in the region of his ancestors, and that today he only goes to Paris in winter. The rest of the time he lives in Gervoissy. *"On revient toujours à ses origines,"* "One always returns to his roots," he explains. He is interested in knowing how I had located him, and what my book is about, the book I mentioned on the telephone: a polite way of getting me to introduce the specific reason I wished to meet him.

I go back to my long and complicated efforts to find him in Paris. After many Gervoises that were not Boileaux, and many Boileaux that were not Gervoises, I made contact with the housemaid of his sister Anne-Marie, who, in the absence of her mistress, kindly offered to give me his number in Gervoissy. Because of my stumbling French, the conversation incorporates bits of other languages, Italian from his side and English or Spanish from mine, in a mixture that produces good results with the help of a few gestures and the mutual acceptance of inevitable gaps. I also explain that I am a professor, here in France for three months to participate in an exchange project between universities in the area of audiovisual arts.

"J'aime bien le cinéma," he says, though he seems unable to remember the last film he saw.

But he comments about the films of his youth with enthusiasm. We talk of Renoir, John Ford, and Eisenstein, of Lang and Chaplin, Valentino and Greta Garbo. We go over *Nosferatu* and *À Nous la Liberté*. We talk of *Camille,* which he watched in his parents' company, in 1935 or 1936—anyway, before the war. For him, the war is an obligatory reference point; time seems to be divided into before and after the war. The expressions *c'était avant la guerre* or *c'était après la guerre* are always coming up in the conversation. (His older brother died in the war.) His only sister, today a widow, was married after the war. The château in Normandy was sold before the war. Greta Garbo was in the audience when *Camille* premiered in Paris before the war. But neither he nor his parents had been able to get close enough for an autograph: she had left immediately after the rounds of applause that filled the theater. And so, they make films in Brazil?

He thanks me for my invitation to attend some of the films from the selection I'm showing at the Sorbonne with moderate success, noting in tiny handwriting the address, dates, and times. I speak a little about each film and he listens attentively. Based on my synopses, he underlines *Memórias de Helena* and *Como Era gostoso meu Francês*. But he advises, politely, that he will not be able to attend any of them. Paris, only in the winter. Nevertheless, he meticulously folds up the paper with its notations and puts it in his jacket pocket. That done, he lifts an amiable gaze to me. The last chords of the overture have sounded, and it's time for me to raise the curtain and bring Guilhermina onto the scene. The waiter serves us another round. We toast each other, *"Santé, santé. Au cinéma, au cinéma."*

Yes, I explain, among other things I am also a writer in my spare time. Filmmaking in Brazil is no easy matter, and being a professor doesn't keep me fed. At the moment, I'm fulfilling a

———

request of my editor, who asked me to put together the biography of a Brazilian woman of some importance, a personage unknown up to now who suddenly surfaced from the past. It's my first biographical work and I'm still gathering material. I follow this tack.

Chin resting on the backs of his hands, which are propped on the cane, the old gentleman listens to me curiously, waiting to find out what I'm getting at and, more particularly, how he fits into the picture. We approach Guilhermina slowly, like two spaceships that float serenely in transcendental dimensions, I coming from Planet Earth and knowing where I'm going, he with eyes closed, forgotten on Mars. Sitting on an asteroid at some other point in space, Guilhermina waits, probably filing her fingernails. But there is something in the old man's eyes that begins to change very slowly. It is a most subtle change in their color; they turn imperceptibly from blue to a tone bordering on light gray, then darken and become opaque. His head separates itself gradually from his cane, his body straightens as if sensing the heat from a meteorite only seconds away from its impact. In the instant that my last words and his gaze converge on the same point in time and space, my listener has already turned to rock. His voice is suddenly cold and harsh as he asks,

"What did you say her name was?"

"Guilhermina," I repeat. "Don't you remember her? A young woman, fair skinned, very red hair, about twenty-four or twenty-five years old at that time. She stayed with your family."

"You're mistaken."

"*C'était avant la guerre. . . .*"

"*N'insistez pas, Monsieur, vous vous êtes trompé.*" ("Don't insist, sir, you are mistaken.")

He gets up, grabs his cane, and leaves without another word. Before he closes the door, with both feet already in the street, he turns one last time in my direction, as though seeking confirmation of some sort. And with a look that banishes me to whatever hell I came from, he slams the door. The waiter exchanges two words with the *patronne* who is wiping glasses behind the counter. Both of them look at me distrustfully. *Ces étrangers* . . . and they shake their heads sadly.

Chapter Twenty-one

Patrick never forgave Guilhermina for our brother's death. It's very hard to lose an older brother, especially when you're only seventeen."

The lady before me murmurs these words with a smile of understanding for the childish sentiments of those we love, sentiments that demand particular tolerance from us. Her eyes analyze me for a moment, as if trying to discover my range of knowledge about a subject she knows in depth: the human soul. It is obvious I fail the test. But on this rainy, interminable afternoon, I am preferable to rereading some old magazine or watching the rerun of *War and Peace* that was on television when the maid announced my arrival half an hour earlier.

"Can you tell me why?"

"Yes, of course," she sighs, almost worn out from managing such a story alone. But she stays silent.

"Did your brother Jean–Marc die in the war?"

"Let's say he killed himself in the war. *C'est différent, n'est-ce pas?*"

I agree that it is. Better to agree with my hostess. From the tone of her voice on the telephone, I had already sensed that possible points of divergence should be kept to the essential minimum.

The maid serves tea with two tiny loaves of bread. *"Ils sont cuits à la maison,"* ("They are baked here,") Anne-Marie explains as she blows on hers and nibbles it as a squirrel would an acorn.

"So you knew Guilhermina, Madame?"

"Of course, we were friends. My two brothers were madly in love with her, but at heart Guilhermina felt more at home with me. We were alike and we enjoyed each other's company. We often went out together. I knew a lot about her, in spite of being younger—good heavens, how old was I then? Fifteen, sixteen?"

"It was before the war."

"Yes, long before, we're talking about 1934 or 1935, at the latest. Guilhermina (she pronounced it *Guiyeirmeen*) couldn't have been more than twenty-five or twenty-six. *Elle était tout à fait ravissante.* (She was absolutely ravishing.) Imagine a widow so young and so desirable. The men went crazy, strangers paid her attentions large and small on any pretext—in the streets, in restaurants, in the subway. I learned, many years later, that a composer had dedicated a sonata to her. At theaters, she would receive passionate notes or small flowers inside boxes of bonbons. My own brother spent hours writing endless poems in praise of her red hair."

"Patrick?"

"No, the older one, Jean-Marc, the one who died in the war. . . ."

"But this reaction of your younger brother Patrick, after so many years, not even wanting to discuss her when I asked . . ."

"Un enfantillage, an overreaction. Who knows, maybe just jealousy mixed with guilt. When someone dies, the most routine events change color. And what may have been vaudeville often becomes tragedy in the minds of more sensitive persons. It's hard to say, after so many years. One day if I get a chance I'll ask Patrick about it. We hardly see each other nowadays. He hardly ever comes to Paris except in the winter, when I travel to Spain. But he did suffer a lot with his brother's pain, that much is certain. Of the three of us, he was always the most sensitive."

"With his brother's pain?"

"Yes, when Guilhermina left us. One day she simply went away and never came back. Or if she came back, she never tried to get in touch with us again. Jean-Marc almost went crazy, he stopped eating, didn't talk to anyone. And Patrick didn't know what to do to relieve his brother's pain. Since she had left only the vaguest indication as to where she was going, Jean-Marc searched the entire city of Paris looking for people who would give him hints about her whereabouts in Italy. And he always came back empty-handed, discouraged, and depressed. But as he retraced the circuits Guilhermina had followed, he must have discovered certain things. . . . *On ne sait jamais, n'est-ce pas?* (One can never know, can they?) He even let his canary die of hunger. *(Vous vous rendez compte?)* You know, they had a more . . . a more personal relationship. Let's say, more intimate. In short, *en un mot,* they slept together."

Here she gives a small shrug, as though disposed to pardon weaknesses committed in the past, especially since they involve persons already dead, whose memory, when all is said and done, should be respected. No problem, as far as I'm concerned. Besides, it all happened before the war.

"I never touched on the subject, because it was something between the two of them. Patrick knew, the servants knew, everyone knew except me and my parents, who chose only to suspect. My parents were always very practical when it came to personal matters. But one night I woke up thirsty and went down to the kitchen for a drink of water. I came upon Patrick crouching behind Jean-Marc's door. I stayed very quiet, trying to guess what was happening. I did, of course. Poor Patrick."

"But why?"

"Have you ever been thirteen? A complicated age, don't you think?"

It is curious for me to hear about the people *around* Guilhermina, as if viewing a painting by looking first at the secondary

---

141

figures. For this reason I avoid centering our conversation more directly on the subject that brings me to the small apartment in Rue Cortambert since I suppose the lady before me has no hurry. But I don't know my hostess: the conversation is soon to take an unexpected turn.

Anne-Marie encourages me to talk about Guilhermina and the reasons that might lead someone to write a book about her. As I did with her brother, I try to place the project on the safe terrain of biography. Stretching the truth a little, I explain that Guilhermina had left some poems, never published, that warranted her descendants' attention when they were discovered. Although they didn't exactly merit publication—they were only noteworthy if analyzed in the context of her era and, that understood, were of some value—the poems had spurred the reading of Guilhermina's diaries and voluminous correspondence. These papers, forgotten in the remotest of trunks, had revealed the existence of a singular thinker, given the era.

Just like Patrick before her, Anne-Marie straightens up in her armchair opposite me, except that in her eyes the flame of curiosity and of anticipated pleasure shines. The old lady lets out a *tiens . . .* she seems fascinated by my project. If I play my cards right and season my story with details that sound honest and truthful to her ears, I may deserve a second cup of tea and even another piece of bread.

So I begin to discourse in my heroic and catatonic French about my perception of Guilhermina, a woman brought up with the limitations and the prejudices that prevailed among the families in the interior of my country in the first decades of the century. I explain what a miracle it was that a social class by definition complacent and cowardly could have produced such a remarkable human being. But I make it clear that Guilhermina had not been exactly a pioneer. On the contrary, our country had produced its share of female painters, writers, musicians, and thinkers, a minority carrying on in a predominantly masculine generation, but present

nevertheless. In Guilhermina's case, the amazing thing was the *absence* of some body of work.

In the conventional sense of the word, I explain, Guilhermina had not been an artist. Nor had she left behind anything that could be considered a cultural legacy. She wasn't a revolutionary focused on social issues—her interest in matters of this sort was phenomenally lacking. Moreover, with the exception of her sparse poems, she had left nothing that revealed the intention or desire to be remembered. One could not say, as sometimes happens, that her life was synonymous with her work. Her life *had been* her work. So who was this woman? With whom had she spent her time? What obstacles had she overcome? From whence sprang the raw material for so many fascinating memories? What was genuine and what was false in her life?

The solution was to investigate. From the entries in her diary, from notations made in the margins of correspondence she received (in which she commented on, with fine irony, the criticism or praise directed at her) it seemed clear that the four years immediately after her first widowhood, her years in Europe, had been vital to her intellectual formation. Particularly since almost nothing had remained from other periods. As she had broken off contact with her family very early, there was only the briefest record of her childhood. There was some material to illuminate her first marriage, less about the second, and virtually nothing about her life as an older woman, when she had sold everything, bought a farm, and retired to a remote part of her country. With the exception of a great-niece, whom she had befriended in the last years of her life, no relative or friend could give an account of her. All in all—and this was the principal challenge for any biographer—she seemed rather like a fictitious character. A biography of her would run the understandable risk of being viewed with reserve or even suspicion.

Anne-Marie listens to me carefully. But all through my spiel, she follows her own trail of memories, like one searching for supporting points in an internal archive to reinforce and confirm everything she hears. Her eyes are turned on me, but I merit only a residual part of their gaze, which travels through other times, other settings. For this reason she is probably as surprised as I with the revelation she blurts out:

"You are aware, of course, that she killed a man."

Faced with my complete shock and worried at her possible indiscretion, she asks more softly:

"You didn't know?"

For a good while we remain mute, facing each other. I lift my cup and ask for more tea. She serves me and adds, as if speaking to herself:

"A rather interesting man, actually."

"Did she tell you about it?"

"Yes . . . and no."

It's her turn to speak, her paths we travel this time. (Who am I to open my mouth now?) Her words reveal the spirit of observation of a woman eager to review an important part of her life. She gives me the impression—as often happens when I talk to people of a certain age—that time is short and therefore the facts can no longer be manipulated or distorted. Furthermore, my hostess is French, cartesian, objective, concise, thin, and angular like the two little rolls the maid serves us again. I devour mine in silence while I listen. I feel like a vampire chained to a time machine: I feed on other people's memories. Curiously enough, my French doesn't even constitute a barrier. I understand almost everything she says, as if I were being pulled through the domain of language by the very force of her words.

Chapter Twenty-two

The bucolic landscape is the same one I saw on my ill-starred attempt to talk with Patrick Gervoise-Boileau, but now it is Easter, 1934. Guilhermina strolls through the fields with Anne-Marie and talks of her marriage to the Honorable. She explains the reasons that had induced her family to marry her off to a man so much older than she was. A man of great possessions and, in his own way, fascinating. A man who had traveled much and attracted beautiful women, who liked to eat and drink well, who was secure in conducting business and whose vision of the world was fundamentally open-minded. A man who had been slender and strong when young, and still bore traces of grace and strength in his soul and memory. A man who had flown in a zeppelin, collected lead soldiers, read very few books, married late in life, had no children, been widowed during a picnic, and exchanged a few parcels of land for a second bride. A man who had spent his evenings playing chess with his only friend and who never went to bed without giving his dog a biscuit.

Arms about each others' waists, picking flowers and braiding them into their hair, the two young women had talked much and exchanged many ideas on their long walks. But Anne-Marie listened to Guilhermina's stories about her married years with reserve, for the difference in age between the husband and wife seemed absurd to her. Since she was at an age when love is usually associated with youth and strength, she thought her cousin, now a widow, was making peace with her past, retouching what had probably been a heavy and somber picture. However, as she was very well bred, she kept her doubts hidden. Or maybe she was not conscious of them.

But one night Guilhermina, who shared a bedroom with her cousin, had had a nightmare and had shouted two or three sentences in Portuguese. Anne-Marie, who didn't understand what she was saying, was much alarmed and tried to calm her cousin, murmuring a few words in French, and it was in French that Guilhermina, still asleep, had dragged her husband's body from a wine cellar to the middle of the bedroom.

"Oui, je l'ai tué, dans une cave, et ça m'a fait grand plaisir de le tuer. Pendant cinquante jours et cinquante nuits je l'ai eu entre mes mains et je l'ai tué très lentement . . ." ("Yes, I killed him, in a cellar, and it gave me great pleasure to kill him. For fifty days and fifty nights I had him in my grasp, and I killed him very slowly. . . .")

The sentences that followed, Anne-Marie understood less clearly. There were references to bars and supplications, and Guilhermina burst out laughing—but what Anne-Marie had heard, once her initial surprise was over, had been enough. Especially because, as soon as she had delivered this burden of speech, Guilhermina relapsed into the soundest of sleep. The laughter and the words she screamed so quickly might have even gone by unnoticed, if it weren't for the relieved slumber that had followed the confession. It was the contrast between sound and silence that had given Anne-Marie a clue to the importance of this incident.

After that night, Anne-Marie began to pay very special attention to each word Guilhermina spoke concerning her past. Like a second camera that shows the same scene from another angle—revealing, in the process, something formerly concealed—Anne-Marie registered her new perspectives. And while the sound track spoke of life, flowers, and harmony, her eyes now discerned shadows amid the light.

"You see, *I knew*. And naturally she couldn't have supposed that I knew. All of a sudden our conversations became unbalanced, except that this time it was in my favor. Everything she continued to tell me about her husband, on our walks through the fields, now took on a different color. Her tenderness and affection for him gained an air of truth, because *he* had believed they were true: otherwise, he might have still been alive. What had seemed to me fussily sentimental up to then, and almost incomprehensible to a European mind, gained in dignity and coherence. The couple had existed; the relationship had been quite real in form but fundamentally truncated in essence. But I still didn't know why. I started asking her lots of questions, trying to open cracks that would permit me to understand her motives. Was it for money? For love of another man? For revenge? And if so, how could she talk of that husband with a tenderness that sounded so evident and sincere to me? Thus I gradually began to realize that there was also a lot of light amid the shadows. And that she had genuinely loved that man."

"And didn't you want to let her know that . . ."

"That I knew? When I exhausted all the resources of my poor little arsenal of questions, limited as I was by the dimensions of my supposed ignorance, I considered doing just that—telling her about the nightmare—but I didn't have time. One afternoon she packed her bags and cut off the magic of the moment. On the train to Paris I thought of taking up the matter again, but the opportunity didn't arise. I actually believe she sensed something in the air, sensed I was on the trail of something. The fact is she escaped from me, like a bird that flies quickly upward and lights on another branch. *'Un tout petit oiseau aux cheveux rouges,'* ('A tiny little bird with red hairs') as Jean-Marc called her in one of his poems . . ."

I miss Andrea's presence here at my side. Or rather, I intuitively feel the lack of what she probably knows or senses about this part of the story. For I myself have nothing to offer as a counterpoint to what is being told to me. It is possible that Anne-Marie perceives my difficulty, for she pauses a little, gives me a piercing glance, and asks:

"You mentioned some diaries. Didn't she leave anything in them about the death of her husband? Or about what he was like? To me, he seemed like a rather interesting man, with his money, his plantations, his slaves, his adventures, his passions as an adolescent, his love for Maria Stella."

"Did you know Maria Stella?"

"Of course, we are—or rather, we were—cousins. Don't forget that both the Maia Macedo family as well as the Gervoise-Boileau are Rinaldo di San Rufo on their respective maternal sides. I myself am the godchild of Maria Stella's oldest daughter, Francesca. Whom I haven't seen for years, incidentally; but she's a person you should perhaps look up. Of course, Maria Stella died many years ago. She died . . ."

"Before the war?"

"Just before. We didn't go to her ninetieth birthday party as we had planned, because my father had passed away shortly before that and we were still in mourning. That was in 1936 and she died not long afterward—but you're right, it was before the war. I only knew Maria Stella slightly. I saw her a few times when I was a child. On one of her trips to Paris she stayed with us. I was quite small, probably not more than eight years old, and she was already quite elderly, traveling with a young manservant who followed her everywhere like a shadow, carrying her bags, her jewelry box, and her papers. A manservant who, according to Patrick, gave her back-rubs when she bathed. She was quite a personage, Maria Stella . . . I can still hear her strident voice greeting me one afternoon when I went down to the salon to meet her. *'Chèrrre Anne-Marie!'* she exclaimed, rolling her *r*'s as Italians always do, and waving her jeweled arms, leaving my clothes saturated with the smell of her perfume for days. They said that she had been ravishingly beautiful when she was young; I don't know. Guilhermina told me that she almost drove Carlos Augusto crazy . . . yes, that's quite probable. Some women have that power, and Maria Stella might have been one. Guilhermina certainly was. When my parents spoke of Maria Stella, they always exchanged a meaningful look which didn't escape me."

"And Carlos Augusto, did your parents ever meet him? They were more or less contemporaries, weren't they?"

"Oh no, my parents were much younger, and that was precisely what made it so hard for me to conceive of Guilhermina's marriage—a girl not much older than I was, married to a man older than my own parents . . . no, they never met, there was never an opportunity. My parents occasionally referred to some vague Brazilian relatives, with whom they exchanged Christmas cards and so forth, but nothing more than that, as I recall."

She falls silent for an instant, as if suddenly remembering something.

"And yet, it was Maria Stella herself . . . Once I overheard a conversation between her and my mother, in which they were discussing those *Brazilian relatives* of ours. Both of them seemed to be very amused at Carlos Augusto's provincialism. He had by mistake called the *villa patrizia* in which Maria Stella and Raffaele lived, near Salerno, a castle, when everyone knows that castles, strictly speaking, don't exist in that part of Italy. Maria Stella told my mother that our Brazilian cousin, in his youthful enthusiasm, always had a certain tendency to idealize everything he saw, *including her*—and at that point they started whispering and giggling together. But when I came into the room, they quickly changed the subject, praising my dress at the top of their lungs."

She smiles at me and together we relive the scene. Serious again, she proceeds:

"But aside from that, I don't remember lengthy comments about Carlos Augusto. Thus it was quite a surprise for my parents to receive a letter from Guilhermina thanking us for our condolences

———

upon the death of her husband and announcing her visit to Paris. 'Hey, our Brazilian cousin will soon be visiting,' my father exclaimed when he opened the letter one evening before dinner. With that, the Brazilian cousin was in spirit among us as we dined that night. We suddenly all talked about Brazil, a place more remote to us than Africa, where at least we had colonies, and our family, property. If today we still hardly have an idea of your country, imagine back then! . . . Anyway, what mattered was the cousin, not the country. What would she be like? How would she behave? We knew she was much younger than her late husband. I remember quite well that Patrick whispered things into Jean-Marc's ear, boys' talk, things about which girls know a lot, but say little.''

Here, another glance at me to make certain I have understood her meaning.

"But I'll never forget our amazement when, two months later, Guilhermina entered the hall of our house (back then our family lived in a *hôtel particulier* in Avenue Geor—ah, you know?) and we realized that she was almost a girl. She had bought a beret when she got off the ship in Marseille and braided her hair down her back, a long red braid that reached almost to her waist. If, instead of a small trunk and two suitcases, she had carried a book bag and books, we would have sworn she was a Parisian schoolgirl knocking on our door to sell us raffle tickets for her lycée's charity bazaar.''

A new silence. I hear a small noise to my right, as if a child or a little animal were scratching at the door. *"Les chiens vous dérangent?"* ("Do dogs bother you?") my hostess inquires amiably as she gets up. Nothing bothers me—and, when the door is open, a poodle comes in, gives me a rapid sniff, and jumps up onto Anne-Marie's lap. We talk a little about pets, dogs and cats, and the maid comes in to turn on the lights and close the curtains. It's the hour when husbands come home from work, but I can tell there's no husband in this house. I breathe in the air of availability of someone

who lives alone with her impeccably uniformed maid and her beribboned poodle. The maid asks if she should light the fireplace. Anne-Marie inquires if I would care for a drink now.

"Mathilde, the gentleman will have a cognac. I will have a whiskey."

With the fire burning brightly in the fireplace and a glass of cognac in my hands, I slide deeper down into my armchair and begin to speak of Guilhermina as I have grown accustomed to envision her. I bring to light her childhood photos found in the hatbox (*"Ça alors,"* exclaims Anne-Marie, when I mention the tag from the SS *Manitoba* on the outside—and comments that she herself had crossed the Atlantic on that very ship). I speak of the photos, the letters, the black mask from a masquerade ball, the arranged marriage, the nuptial rape—"Oh! That's why she did it! How terrible!,"—of the seven years of waiting, of her sinuous movements with her husband, of Flávio Eduardo and his library (*"C'est vrai, elle m'a beaucoup parlé de ce personnage"*) ("That's true, she spoke a lot about this character"), of the wine cellar and its silences, but, throughout all this, I talk with equal emphasis of Guilhermina's mental windows, ever open to other worlds and other landscapes. . . .

I also tell Anne-Marie what I know about Guilhermina's years in Europe—and I mention I have heard a little about her, Anne-Marie, and her parents and brothers. She listens to me with great interest. As we review this period together, I discover that it was in Anne-Marie's company that Guilhermina had gone to the Salle Gaveau the night she met Paul Nat (*"Oui, j'étais là, il m'a offert un chocolat . . ."*), and when I unveil what would yet occur between the two of them later on, she almost dumps the poodle off her lap (*"C'est pas vrai!"* she exclaims incredulously, *"elle l'a revu?"*). I suddenly realize that Anne-Marie is fishing for facts and completely in my hands if she wants to know the story. Her attention is a measure of the fascination that Guilhermina holds for her. But to bring things back into balance and show she isn't in such a hurry, she returns to the entrance hall of the *hôtel particulier*.

"My parents had planned to go and bring Guilhermina home from the station, but she had taken time out to visit the Château d'If and had missed the earlier train from Marseille. From our first conversation with her, over the telephone, we had understood she was arriving in the afternoon, but we were wrong. When the doorbell rang and the servants came to announce that *'la jeune dame brésilienne était arrivée,'* we all rushed down to greet her."

Chapter Twenty-three

Guilhermina became one of the family almost immediately. Besides being genteel, well-mannered, and sweet, she possessed an inner serenity that radiated from her whole being. When she said something, no matter how simple, her words had the ring of truth. When she looked at people, she stared directly into their eyes. She seemed to guess what we tried to dissimulate, we with our tired blood, our guillotines, our eight centuries of parlor games. When she spoke of her country, she made us *see* the landscapes so clearly, almost as if we were there. I have no idea if her descriptions were accurate or not—and they may even have been invented. But for us, they were true. And so, although she was very young, she captivated our family and friends without much effort. Today it's simple for me to understand why: she had killed a man! And with just cause! A person who passes through something like that gains a type of authority that we mere mortals can't achieve in fifty years. My husband always said—oh, it's too bad you couldn't have met my husband, he was so fond of Guilhermina . . ."

"Really?"

"Ah, my poor husband . . ."

Here she sighs so deeply that the poodle automatically licks her hand. This little dog . . . The maid serves a new round of drinks without being asked. I should have chosen vodka, for I get the feeling that social and geographical barriers are about to crumble and we're going to get plastered right here in the middle of the sixteenth *arrondissement*. But I accept another cognac. The maid puts more wood on the fire, leaves the bottles on the little table beside her mistress, asks permission to leave, *"bonsoir madame, bonsoir monsieur,"* and closes the door. Through the echo of Anne-Marie's sigh I hear the remote sound of the street door closing somewhere to the rear. Lulled as I watch the flames rise toward the chimney, I sink deeper into my recollections and I again see the shadows on the walls of my own apartment a few months ago, when Andrea, dining by candlelight, had spoken to me at length and in detail about her aunt Guilhermina. In the wake of those memories, I return to the steps that lead down to the old cellar. Silver candelabra in his right hand, the Honorable descends them with Guilhermina, looking for an obscure bottle of liqueur, navigates among sea foam, Arabian horses, and turbans, until, lying on three sacks of rice, he finally surrenders himself to his two women.

Thus, I am surrounded by Guilhermina and the whole Gervoise-Boileau clan, as well as Andrea, the Honorable, Maria Stella, and the old Baron Rafaele di San Rufo. It's no accident that the dog, with the wisdom of the truly enlightened, suddenly grows agitated and barks a few times, looking restlessly about. Anne-Marie reassures it, patting its head absently. The gesture and the new sigh she heaves postpone all my characters' entrance onstage, for now the whole living room is taken up by a beloved husband who waits patiently for the words of sympathy I am supposed to pronounce.

"Yes, your brother told me that you had recently been widowed. . . ."

"One of the best men on earth, my husband," she murmurs, eyes lost in the flickering firelight. But at once she livens up again, straightening her body and giving a little shake, as if to banish all sadness. Her sentences emerge clear, logical, direct, weighed and measured with cartesian exactitude.

"Of course, he always had his head in the clouds, he was far from having any practical sense, and in financial matters he was a disaster. For those reasons my parents had opposed our marriage. He was very poor. Although he was a remote relation of ours, he was almost destitute. And"—maternal smile—"there was the problem of the balloons, too. . . ."

"Balloons?"

It's my turn to bring a dead person close to our fireplace and hers to be surprised:

"Was he by any chance Danish?"

"How did you know?" she asks, drawing in her breath.

I explain that his name—Peter, if I am correct?—had appeared in Guilhermina's diaries, but only in passing, as one of the guests at a dinner party offered by her parents shortly after her arrival. According to the only reference she made, he was Danish and he loved balloons. That was all. Anne-Marie closes her eyes in an effort to recall the scene and realizes that it was true—and that, at fifteen, she had not even noticed the presence, at that table, of the man she was to marry ten years later. She is completely surprised. It's as if, by chance, a file drawer had opened before her eyes, offering precious material about a time that preceded her own happiness.

"*Mon dieu, c'est pourtant vrai,*" she murmurs to herself in wonder. She serves herself a generous dose of whiskey without bothering to offer me more cognac. (We have achieved this level of intimacy; from now on, it's up to me to look after my own glass.) But she now frowns, puts the dog on a pillow beside her, and leans toward the fireplace, as if warming her memories in its flames. I myself make an effort to accompany her, since I know almost nothing of the scene in which she is immersed, except that maybe they had eaten. . . .

"*. . . du faisan!*" she exclaims suddenly. And smiles at me, very proud of her recollection: "We ate pheasant that night, I re-member very well. We were all watching Guilhermina, my broth-ers in particular, to see how she behaved at table. It was our first big dinner with her and not only did she conduct herself with absolute poise, she also discoursed about types of game, white meat and dark meat, compared the game on her plantation with what she hoped to taste in Europe, complimented us on the truffles and the subtle-ties of our wines . . . and Peter (good grief, how extraordinary), seated beside her, talking about balloons—he never talked about anything else. I think a few days later he even took her for a ride in one of them . . . ah, Peter, how I miss him . . . always in the clouds, wearing his little red-and-white cap. . . ."

She stops and gazes at me, vivacious and passionate. Indeed, it's another woman who talks with me now, eyes shining intensely.

"Naturally my parents forbade me even to think about going for a balloon ride with him, especially since he was an 'older man.' I was fifteen at that time, he was thirty-two. Imagine . . . I actually never even looked at him in those days, nor he at me. Yes, I was fifteen . . . how amazing to remember him at that table . . . of course, he had always frequented our house as a sort of poor rela-tion. My father used to say that he came to us for his only decent meal of the week. Poor dear. He lived in Saint-Cloud. Think of it, his only meal of the week! My father always was cruel, but probably he wasn't far from the truth. Peter spent all he had on his balloons, and he had so little . . . just think, his room was on the sixth floor and the hotel naturally didn't have an elevator. He was embarrassed because, from the fourth floor up, the rug on the staircase was threadbare. After the fifth, the ceilings were only half as high, and there was no rug at all."

The drinks are beginning to have the effect of softening the outlines of the people and objects in her memory, as well as the words on her lips. Slowly her finger traces the shape of a balloon in the air. Once it materializes before us, she produces the information we were lacking to complete the scene and give it the final documentary touch.

"He even named one of his first balloons after her, *Guilhermina I.* It was green and yellow, the colors of your country's flag, I believe? I remember that my parents were quite impressed with this. But by then Guilhermina had already left for Italy, and I don't think she ever knew of this honor paid to her. You see, it's one more example of the fascination she held for people, since I don't believe they saw each other more than once or twice." (Here, a short pause.) "No, I don't think so. . . ."

A fragment of thought seems to make her frown for an instant, but the sun at once reappears from behind the clouds and she continues her smiling journey through the skies.

"We began to see each other and go out together, Peter and I, when I entered the university . . . my parents were against it, of course. Peter made fun of them a little. Once he told me it was very restful to talk to my father, because he was a man who always gave one the impression that the axis of the world somehow depended on the quality of his bedroom curtains. *Papá* heard about this, grew furious, and naturally forbade Peter ever to set foot in our house again."

She laughs, pleased with this memory.

"Nevertheless, we fell in love. We went everywhere together, stuck to each other like glue. Of course I finally took up ballooning too. *Et pour cause* . . . I can't even tell you. . . ."

A more private moment follows, with a long, mysterious smile that only the poodle can decipher, wagging its tail happily and earning a new caress, this time full of enthusiasm and affection. Anne-Marie motions me to help myself to more cognac and serves herself another dose of whiskey. She is full of energy, as if her airborne husband were within her. And so he is.

"He's the one who taught me to like this poison! Imagine, whiskey! Only the finest wines and champagnes were served in my parents' house. But nobody's perfect . . . and a little drink isn't so bad, after all. Oh, life is so strange . . . to think I owe to Guilhermina, in a way, the courage to have married against my parents' wishes. . . ."

She laughs again softly. We both laugh. We are happy with the surprises life always has in store. We are happy with our drinks. We're slightly tipsy.

"How come you owe this to Guilhermina?"

Anne-Marie grins at me. Now she is the true mistress of the story. After all, what real interest could she have had in what happened to Guilhermina before or after that period? None, or very little. On the level of *faits divers,* maybe. But not as far as her own life goes. What matters, in her eyes, is what happened in those two or three months in 1934. The rest is really my problem. But she feels good: after all, the night is young and the memories, still warm and generous, dance in her mind.

"She made me read the right books."

She looks at me and I once again feel I am being examined, as if she were now evaluating my degree of familiarity with the implications of such matters for an adolescent in the formative stages. I pass the test; after all, I'm a writer. Probably a good one, since I can handle my drinks.

"She made me read Balzac and George Sand, Flaubert and Stendhal. She regretted I didn't know Portuguese to be able to acquaint myself with the best authors of her country, whose works she described to me. She explained that there was nothing wrong with the work of, for example, Delly or the Countess of Ségur. Much to the contrary. And that *Slave or Queen?* or *General Dourakine* were books that certainly had their reason for being. But that there existed other ways of seeing the world, other directions for my dreams, other crimes and punishments, so to speak."

Pensively, she smiles, and exclaims:

"And the hell with my tender age! For her, the younger one's eyes were, the sharper the vision and the deeper the effect. She used to say that, at fifteen, it was better to understand a fraction of a great book than the entire works of many members of the Academy. That was how, in one breath, Voltaire sent all the nuns in my girls' school flying. They disappeared into the air, upside down, legs open, habits flapping, as if swept away by a cyclone."

She looks at me to be sure I accompany the happy flight of the nuns of her childhood. Then she proceeds:

"Mind you, I would have arrived at all these authors on my own someday. But not at fifteen. Certainly not as a daughter in the kind of family I came from. Guilhermina showed me the way."

She sips her drink.

"I only began reading these authors immediately after she went away. I stole the books from the shelves of my friends' older brothers, or took them out of libraries in my parents' name, or bought them with money from my allowance . . . and the more Jean-Marc searched for Guilhermina in the streets of Paris, the more I found her again in the pages I read."

She raises her glass, as if to toast something.

"Understand, I was very naive, I saw the world through rose-colored glasses. And Guilhermina, fortunately, had killed a man. Actually, with two or three sentences, two or three books, followed by many others, and that magnificent cadaver which, at the right time *(à la bonne heure)* had emerged from a nightmare, she pointed my life in a whole new direction. If it weren't for her, maybe I might have had to kill a man myself. . . . But it wasn't necessary. Thus I could use my energies for other things, thanks to her. Peter always said that from up in the sky things looked so tiny . . . And she said that, in the end, all drama reduced itself to almost nothing. Each of them was right. Each in his or her own balloon. Everything, seen from up above, grows very tiny indeed. *N'est-ce pas?*"

"*A la vôtre, Anne-Marie!*"

"*A la vôtre, Fernando!*"

Chapter Twenty-four

                        M y work on the university pro-
ject fortunately kept me from being swallowed in the quicksand of
other people's past. Otherwise, I wouldn't have survived my six
weeks in Paris. I was constantly on the go. In the mornings, I over-
saw the projection of films to attentive audiences; in the afternoons
I analyzed scripts or discussed production problems with visual-arts
students. At lunchtime I would jump off the metro and run to see
an exhibit at the Louvre or the Beaubourg. In the evenings after
class, or on weekends, I continued my search for fragments of Guilhermina's life, guided by her presence—when I wasn't shoved
along by her comments and suggestions. All this in a city that is
pure cinema, where yesterday's films are always just on the point of
merging into those of tomorrow. Thus it was among intertwining
images, that I found myself one Sunday afternoon at another of the
addresses rescued from the hatbox, *18 bis, Rue de la Harpe.*

    If it weren't for the McDonald's, the Greek restaurants, and
the sound of a jukebox, the street would have looked like a set from
Marcel Carné, the old six-story buildings leaning gracefully out
over the sidewalks, the pots of geraniums lined up in the windows,
the end of the street fading into infinity, like the backdrop of a stage
studio owners paint to narrow spacial perspectives and costs. The

snarling concierge two steps above my head was real enough, though.

"Vous désirez?"

Unable to give free rein to the expression of my most secret desires *(Je désire, chère madame, vous donner deux ou trois coups de balai aux fesses)* (What I want, madame, is to wallop your backside two or three times with a broom), I smile stoically as I extract from my pocket a small, much-folded clipping, stolen from the past.

"Un petit renseignement, madame . . ." She was really mean.

How good it would be to say what I really want. I want everything, madame: the past, the present, the future, peace, disarmament, you in my bathtub. In this building, when your mother or your grandmother was concierge, lived Marie-France Jocelin, lover of beautiful women and blackmailer of public men, smuggler of green dwarfs and trafficker in white slavery, owner of forbidden cabarets and intimate friend of someone I knew, last seen in Agadir. . . .

"Un simple renseignement, madame . . ."

The clipping is attentively inspected. No good. She shakes her head above me, adding one more *je regrette* to my collection of unsuccessful attempts. The owner? *Monsieur,* the building has belonged to the same owner for more than twenty years. How, *before* that? How long ago do you mean? *1937?! Mais, mon cher Monsieur, franchement . . .* Even a group of children playing near the doorway look at me with a certain alarm. Perhaps the prefecture? The clipping is handed back with a theatrical gesture. Two dry whisks of her broom raise dust, putting an end to the interview. *Au revoir Monsieur.*

Merci Madame. Strolling through this city doesn't exactly constitute a sacrifice. The problem is to find the marks of trails erased by time. The old clipping with the news of the 1937 police raid carries the picture of Marie-France, but makes no reference to the address of her nightclub, only to its section of the city. My walks through the little streets near the Place Clichy and the Place

---

161

Blanche produced no results. Nobody had ever heard of El Bolero. It was, in fact, very remote in time. Now, I must resign myself to the failure of the residential address found in the old envelope full of recipes for seventeenth-century Italian desserts. Too bad. What exactly was I looking for anyway? By this time, Marie-France, who was older than her friend Guilhermina, would probably be dead. So, what was I after? Some descendant? Acquaintance? Room-mate? Very unlikely, so many years later. What then?

"*Monsieur . . .*"

The weak voice barely reaches me.

"*Monsieur . . .*"

Maybe I dropped something? I turn around and time turns around with me. The more contemporary facades, the McDon-ald's, and the Greek restaurants become less distinct, the noise all of a sudden seems subdued, somewhere the sound of an accordion has replaced the jukebox, light itself has dimmed around me, there is less neon glare and more of a crowd in the street, couples stroll arm in arm, some gentlemen even wear hats. . . .

"*Monsieur . . .*"

I can't see anyone calling me—until I discern a child pushing her way toward me between other pedestrians. She's short and chubby, and could be one of the children who were observing my conversation with the concierge a few minutes ago. Yes, I recog-nize her knitted cap and dark green skirt. She walks slowly, making difficult progress against the flow of the crowded sidewalk. The closer she comes, the less she looks like a child. When she finally gets near me, I instinctively put my hands in my pockets; she's a beggar. A yard below me, she smiles.

"*Non, monsieur, il ne s'agit pas de ça.*" ("That's not what I want.")

Her smile is enough for me to remove my hand from my pocket. It's the tired smile of a circus clown, head half-bowed, eyes gentle between her wrinkles. The small body cannot hide her hopes that this moment in the midst of so many tall people will not be prolonged more than strictly necessary. I clear a path for us and we turn off the crowded street to the left, I solicitous and almost curved over her, my arms half-open to protect her from being run into, she marching before me like a penguin. We go into a café and she climbs on a chair. I sit down beside her. The eagle-nosed waiter with a proud look on his face and a towel over his arm addresses me as if my companion didn't exist:

"Monsieur?"

It's up to me to look at her, which I do with the hopefulness of one who holds the most tenuous of threads between his fingers. If she breathes an answer, it's because she exists.

"Une menthe à l'eau. Merci."

I ask for a beer, and the nose and the white towel disappear between the tables. Little by little, the light and sounds return to normal; there is a jukebox here, but it doesn't bother us. The little woman recovers her breath. How old could she be? Between sixty and seventy? Her voice is hoarse and grave.

"I work in that building where you just were."

Perhaps supposing I don't quite understand what she's saying, she mimics a person polishing furniture, and adds,

"I'm in charge of the cleaning. I've worked there for years and years."

She shrugs her shoulders, meaning, *it could be worse*. The waiter leaves our drinks on the table together with the bill, a local habit I find hard to accept. She holds her *menthe* with two hands and takes a little sip, inspecting me closely, as if she too wanted to make sure of my existence.

"I always knew somebody would come."

"Somebody?"

"Yes, somebody. But I expected someone older."

I feel myself transplanted into another story. A story that briefly intersects with mine, and suddenly I see myself sitting here at this table through her eyes. If I don't blink, if I don't say anything too terribly wrong, it's possible that something will transpire. What, I don't know.

"*Vous permettez?*"

She extends a hand toward me, as if I were supposed to present some credentials. I hesitate for a heartbeat, but at once produce the little newspaper clipping, which she unfolds with infinite care. With an enormous, gap-toothed smile, she places her finger on the grainy photo.

"That's me, in the back."

From the stage of her cabaret, Marie-France, body bending forward, hands leaning on her generous half-open thighs, acknowledges the applause of an invisible audience.

"I'm almost directly behind her, the third from right to left."

She winks at me and wags her head as if to say *Those were good times,* and takes a sip of her drink. She holds the glass up to the light, taps it with her finger, and laughs:

"The four of us, all four this color."

I feel I should contribute some remark, to legitimize my participation in this conversation:

"Haven't you ever gone back?"

"Back? . . ."

"To Italy."

"Ah, Italy . . ."

A treasure chest of compacted images passes for a second through her eyes, which smile inwardly upon a sunny past. An oxcart loaded with wheat and peasants crosses the space between us.

"No, Italy is in the past . . . I've been French for fifty years."

Now comes the question which could facilitate or complicate things.

"And where are you from, Monsieur?"

"From Brazil."

"Ah . . ."

———

My nationality is absorbed slowly, along with another sip of her drink. The information is being collated into the dusty old files of some remote archive. An evasive answer is the result.

"Yes . . . of course."

It's my turn to ask a question, which I do, walking on eggs.

"And Marie-France, can you tell me what happened to her?"

I speak as if I were asking for news of some acquaintance from whom I was separated through absolutely mundane circumstances. But the words sound false, as if stolen from another text. I think of the actor who, in a great hurry, dashes into the wrong theater, goes directly on stage, and rattles off his lines to the confused audience of another play. My companion, by contrast, knows her cues and speeches well.

"Marie-France?"

She knows how to pause, too. Taking a deep breath, she places her glass on the table, points her two arms in front of her, takes aim at the street, and shoots the pedestrians from one side to the other.

"Ta-ta-ta-ta-ta!"

"Shot?"

"During the war."

"By the Germans?"

"It was never really clear. It could have been the Germans. What difference does it make?"

"None, of course."

It's an absurd answer, the answer of an intruder into other people's wars. Oh, that war, always present. (Could Marie-France have died on the same day as Jean-Marc?) I don't feel up to stumbling around blindly in the dark. It's my turn to sigh.

"Look, I'm sorry, but I'm not really the person you were waiting for."

"Who was I waiting for?"

"I don't know."

"So?"

"So?"

"How do you know that you're not the person I was waiting for?"

Hearty laughter on both sides. The waiter stops beside us again. He seems intrigued at our merriment. Perhaps he's sorry for having underestimated one individual in this party. It's too late. I inquire with a small gesture if she wants another drink. *Non merci.* I order another beer without even looking at the waiter, who retires, nose wilted, shoulders slumped, towel drooping.

"In truth, I'm more interested in another person."

"I know, I already figured that out. *La Brésilienne . . .*"

"You say that as if it hurt you."

"It was very painful for all of us. One day she simply went away . . . without telling us a word, no note, nothing . . ."

The small body stretches up on the chair, her short arms open, and she exhales deeply, as if to inject a breath of life into the past.

"She used to play with us as if we were four dolls."

"Dolls?"

The look she gives me signifies: *Why not? Can't you picture me as a doll?* But there is more tolerance than impatience in her words.

"Yes, like dolls. She took care of us, helped us to dress. It was hard for us to change clothes behind the stage between numbers, in the dark, night after night. . . . She was very clever with her hands. She sewed all our green plumes back on the dresses. She had very pretty hands. Did you know her?"

"No. Well, yes and no. A little."

"Red hair, soft-spoken, a mischievous intelligence. And distinctive—I don't know exactly why. She had lived, that much was certain. What her life had been like, no one knew. Once when we were rummaging through one of her bags, we discovered a mysterious silver pistol. Marie-France was the opposite; she was cruel to us. She had experienced much too, but stupid things. Things that had made her into a petty, malicious woman. Before Guilhermina

———

166

joined us, she used to beat us. And sometimes she would chain us up to the bedposts.''

"Chain you up?"

"At night, when she went out with her friends, she would leave all four of us together, handcuffed to the bedposts in the hotels where we were staying.''

"And didn't you complain?"

"To whom? We had no papers, no money, the police were always after us, or at least that was what Marie-France gave us to understand . . .''

Her voice drops. "Chained to the bed . . .''

Her two small fists close on the surface of the table and her face darkens.

"And on top of that we had to watch what they did on that bed when they got back from their nights on the town!''

Something has been lost in transition. A sudden cut, a suppressed scene—and what was affection has turned to hatred. Her head is cocked to one side, the look in her eyes pierces mine like a blade.

"They were beautiful, those two women, and they drove us mad. The more they drove us mad, the wilder they became themselves. I hated the whole thing. We used to shake our chains over the two of them, we shook our chains over the bed.''

She shakes her arms above her head, her small body swinging perilously on the chair. The couples sitting near us register the scene without understanding it. The confession, in a low voice, doesn't take long to follow.

"But the truth is, I never felt so alive.''

I try, in a voice equally low, to guide the conversation back into more tolerable areas. I feel like an old priest with rounded shoulders and dark robes, rubbing his hands lasciviously inside the confessional as he demands to hear more.

"But wasn't Guilhermina good to you four?''

"Yes, when she wasn't driven crazy . . . when the other one didn't make her crazy, she was . . ."

Her thumb and forefinger rub together, both coming close to her nose in a rapid sniffing gesture, head spinning backward.

"You understand, at times they went for strange things . . . and acted very wild . . . very wild . . ."

She laughs, moving her head back and forth, eyes closed, her short legs swinging on the chair. Then she takes a deep breath and suddenly grows calm again. She looks at me with a serene air, faintly worried:

"Are you surprised?"

"No, not at all."

Which is true. There's no time for surprises. I take up the conversation again from a new angle:

"They met on a train."

"I know, I know all about the train, I've heard a thousand times about the train, the steam rising from the consommé, the champagne, the sparkling conversation . . . Marie-France was capable of seducing a fencepost. With us, when she brought us to France from Italy—two or three years before the Brazilian woman showed up—there was a train, too. Except, that time, we traveled separately, she in first class, and we in third, almost as if we were baggage. Which we were, in a way."

I breathe more easily; apparently we are back in the domain of bearable memories.

"I'll never forget that trip."

Chapter Twenty-five

W e were girls of fifteen or sixteen, four virgin dwarfs obtained at random on the other side of the border. Marie-France had gotten two of us from a circus in Palermo. The other two, my cousin and I, came from small villages in Tuscany. I was exchanged for a basketful of strawberries and some cream, and a few coins for my parents. The four of us traded for peanuts, in an operation made official by a piece of paper that was probably worthless, and that we never saw again."

She seems to feel hot. Removing her beret, she places it on the table. Her hair, surprisingly long and still blond, falls in curls over her shoulders. She gives her head a shake and the journey continues.

"It was the first time we had ever traveled, by train or anything else that moved. That in itself united the four of us forever. Marie-France put us in third class and walked off down the platform to the first-class cars. All four of us hung out the window of the train, looking at that woman who had promised us riches and fame and now distanced herself from us with quick steps, balancing on incredibly high heels. All of a sudden a huge jet of steam spurted out from the train right beside her and she disappeared entirely from our sight, as if swallowed by a white cloud. We had never seen anything like that. And the whistles and noise on all sides! We thought she had died. The car heaved, throwing us to the floor, and the train began to move. We spent the night in terror, all four of us mute and huddled together on our bench, eating nothing, talking to no one, not even going to the bathroom. We were only reassured at the end of the line, fifteen hours later, when we saw her huge red mouth again, smiling at the door."

She laughs her gap-toothed chuckle, eyes almost closed, and looks at me to see if the story amuses me too. With one finger she twirls her beret on the tabletop.

"So, two years of a new life flew by. Some things were bad for us, like the whippings, the chains, and not getting much to eat. Others were good, like our tours through the countryside, the applause, and the coins people threw onto the stage. And sometimes it was good and bad at the same time, like the strawberries and cream brought by serious-looking men with long mustaches. During that time, our families wrote from the other side of the white mountains to confirm that they had received the money we sent them, and to ask for more. They always asked for more. Many years later, when they stopped asking, one after the other, we realized they had finally started to die off."

Her eyes die a little too. The years of demands and resentments had been many.

"On that trip when they met, you weren't along, or were you?"

"No, we never left France again. When Marie-France traveled, which happened once or twice a year, we would work in a circus owned by her cousin. None of us ever left France. And it's too late now, I'm too old to travel and the other three are dead. The last of them, my cousin, died ten years ago. I'm the last survivor. People like us don't usually live to be old; a question of bone mass. I don't know how I lived this long. And I'm still working, too. After the cabaret finally closed and Marie-France disappeared completely, I stayed around the neighborhood, at our last address.

One day during the war, I heard from an acquaintance that she had been shot. The old owner of our building took a liking to me and gave me a job. Years later, the new owner, who inherited me along with the furniture, helped me get my papers in order. I can't complain."

"And when they left, where did they go?"

"I don't know. I don't even know if they went off together. By then, they didn't seem to be on good terms. Marie-France was extremely jealous. And once in a while Guilhermina would play her a trick or two. There was a young man, a musician, who was always hanging around our hotels. Once when I was crossing the Saint-Michel Bridge I saw the two of them together, embracing. When I commented to Guilhermina about it, she said he was a great composer. But she made me swear to keep quiet."

"And the trips they took together occasionally?"

"Marie-France traveled a lot on business. When they met, she had just gone to buy two elephants for her cousin's circus. The cousin was her partner in El Bolero. Did you see the photos of them riding the elephants?"

"Yes. But I thought those photos were taken in France, I don't know why. Who was the man in white holding the elephants?"

"No, the photos were taken in Istanbul. The man was Edouard, a friend of theirs, a strange fellow we would see from time to time. He often came along on our trips through the interior of France. Whenever money was short, he would turn up and pay the bills. When he came to Paris he would always bring us presents, usually strong perfumes from the Orient. I think he was Algerian or Moroccan. But we didn't like him very much. He would caress us and murmur words we didn't understand."

"Did Guilhermina like him?"

"She said she admired certain specific details about him. She said he was a man capable of always repeating the same gesture when he went out: taking a white handkerchief, moistening it with perfume, and putting it in his suit-coat pocket. It was a simple gesture, but one which, according to her, no one performed better than he did. I asked her how she knew this, since we rarely saw him for more than three days running, and nobody was sure where he lived. She answered that she could tell from the way he combed his hair. Just from the way he combed his hair! And for her, that gesture with the handkerchief—entirely imagined—in some way sanctified everything he might do in the streets or elsewhere. That's how Guilhermina was. She imagined scenes for people. And if they were good scenes, she would develop an incredible tolerance for the people she cast in them."

For a moment she is absorbed in seeing Guilhermina again. I too make an effort to see her once more through the filter of all these visions: Patrick's, his sister Anne-Marie's, and now . . .

"I forgot to ask you your name. I'm Fernando."

"Enchantée. Silvana."

She stretches her short arm across the table and squeezes my hand. We touch glasses again, though hers is empty. Then she leans back in her chair once more, anxious to proceed.

"Handkerchiefs in his suit-coat pocket or no, Edouard had a great deal of authority over both of them. Since neither I nor my three friends spoke French very well at the time, we never knew for certain where that power came from. But you could tell there was something, just from the looks they exchanged when they referred to him. Or when the telephone rang during dinner and it was Edouard. It wasn't fear, but something closer to respect. Something that, when it came to their behavior, was translated into a sort of cautious reserve."

She pauses to reflect on these memories, as if to confirm their accuracy. As she is very small and compact, the pause gains a certain dimension. After a few seconds, she nods as if in agreement with herself, then proceeds in a different direction.

"When the last customers left and the porter closed the front door, sometimes we would all eat dinner together, we four, the two of them, and the musicians, at a big table. Those were good moments, moments of tiredness and relief, especially if the night-club had been full and the performance had gone well. I liked to see the two of them talking, gazing deep into each other's eyes and paying no attention to anyone else, full of a special energy, as if a magnetic field were formed between them. From time to time, Guilhermina would give us a little smile, half hidden. It could mean, *Everything's all right*. Or it could mean, *Don't forget to eat your vegetables.''*

Night has fallen. I accept my third glass of beer. The tables around us are all filled with happy people who have just come out of some matinee. I listen to bits of commentaries about an action film. One man says the story is basically implausible. His girlfriend disagrees vehemently. They are both right. For that reason, they exchange a kiss and a hug. French people kiss each other a lot in public.

"When we were on the road, Edouard always drove the car. To help pass the time, Guilhermina would tell us stories about her country, with its forests full of fierce animals and trees laden with unimaginable fruits. She told us of endless coffee plantations or cacao farms. She would ride in front, squeezed between Edouard and Marie-France, and would spin her tales with her eyes on the rearview mirror to evaluate our reactions and thus regulate the size of her animals and fruits. On these occasions she would also tell us long, long stories of her old husband who had kept slaves on one of his plantations when he was young, which impressed us a great deal. Or she would tell us other things about her parents, who had been small landowners, or about her older brother, whom she de-scribed as a successful attorney in Rio de Janeiro, a city where Toscanini had conducted great orchestras while Negroes danced half-naked through the streets with umbrellas and white wigs. Peo-ple danced a lot in her country at that time, according to what she said. Is it still like that?"

"Sort of . . ."

"It's curious. On account of her, I've always felt close to your country, much closer than to Italy. Italy was the past, a place we couldn't go back to. And France, at that time, wasn't exactly the present, it was good and bad, we lived as semicaptives, in a permanent state of agitation, as if Marie-France had mixed drugs into our food, which she very well might have. But your country, Brazil, was like a window for us, with its jungles, its parrots, its jaguars, and slaves who ran away from the plantations to dance in the cities. I imagined the landscapes and the people Guilhermina had seen in her childhood and adolescence, and I asked questions just so she would describe the obvious in greater detail, as if cows could suddenly have five feet or birds fly backward. I would make her repeat the stories about the plagues of grasshoppers which twice had destroyed her folks' small plantation, almost ruining the whole family. Marie-France often got irritated with me and told me to shut up, but Edouard would snarl 'fous-lui la paix,' and she'd be quiet. In his own way, Edouard often protected us. Especially because, at heart, he too liked to hear the stories Guilhermina told while he drove. It kept him from falling asleep at the wheel."

A faint smile of gratitude passes briefly across her lips, though it doesn't seem to alter the reserve with which she continues to judge her supposed protector.

"So Marie-France would give in, and pout in her corner. But there were times when even she was interested in the stories, like the time Guilhermina told us about the morning of her wedding, when she had crossed a river in a little canoe, holding her gown up to her knees to keep it from getting wet in the muddy water that accumulated in the bottom of the canoe. Everyone in the car was in suspense, silently accompanying that canoe gliding in front of us, Guilhermina standing up in the center of the boat, red hair against the white lace of her dress, her father and brother in dark suits, rowing, her mother helping the daughter balance herself with one hand and carrying the shoes of the whole family on her lap. Since I was from the country myself and had seen lots of brides crossing the

wheat fields wearing their white dresses, preceded by musicians who played the violin or the accordion, I understood that Guilhermina's wedding could have been like that."

The smile that lights up her face stays there for a few instants, until turning into a frank chuckle.

"And then there were the fairy tales she told us."

"Fairy tales?"

"Sometimes, at night, when Marie-France went out to negotiate a contract or supervise the rehearsal of a new number (the El Bolero opened new shows every two weeks), Guilhermina loved to tell us stories about witches, fairy godmothers, and goblins. All four of us would be wide awake, electrified in our beds."

She straightens herself all the way up in her chair, wags her head from side to side like a doll, and blinks her eyes happily.

"In her stories everything always came out right, but it wasn't always the successful characters who were the most . . . the most . . ."

She searches for a specific term. I realize that her vocabulary is exceptionally precise. Furthermore, she emphasizes certain expressions, as if underlining them.

". . . the most *honorable*. We perceived the endings as happy because of *her* happiness as narrator; because of the way she herself clapped her hands at the end of each story. Later, though, when we would re-evaluate the stories among ourselves, we always had doubts about the true meaning of each one of her plots. The big bad wolf might eat up Little Red Riding Hood in the presence of the hunter and with the cooperation of the old grandmother, with whom the hunter had an ambivalent relationship. Puss in Boots, victim of a strange skin disease, was found by Prince Charming in the kitchen of a whorehouse. And so it went. Furthermore, with each new version, the stories grew vaguer as to motivation, and more adorned with details. After long years of apprenticeship and affection, a young orphan girl adopted by a benevolent old wizard locks up her protector in a dungeon and runs away to see the world.

I remember one of the versions of this story in particular, in which the old wizard, a little before his death, sang a long tango, embracing his bars, wishing the heroine good luck. Of course Gardel's tangos were in fashion then in Paris. But a wizard singing tangos was too much, even for people like us!"

She almost falls off the chair, she laughs so hard at her own comment. Still gasping, she asks the waiter for a glass of water.

"Do you perhaps still remember that story in detail?"

"That story? Let's see . . . It began, *During the second terrible plague of the giant grasshoppers* . . . I remember that sentence very well. Hmm . . . The heroine is orphaned because the grasshoppers (which measured almost half a yard each, and never flew in swarms smaller than a good-sized cloud) chew her parents and only brother to death. Then they completely destroy the coffee plantations, houses, and flocks of sheep, being omnivorous. The young orphan girl escapes by hiding behind a shelf full of books, and only comes out when the full moon rises in the sky. There is nothing left of her parents or brother, just a gold chain, a piece of shoe, and a few tufts of blond hair. Even the orphan's dolls are torn to pieces. Among them, however, a new doll strangely materializes, a bigger and more richly dressed doll than any that had ever belonged to her. Are you sure you really want to listen to all this?"

"Yes."

She takes two sips of water from the glass the waiter has placed before her, and goes on.

"The doll is magic, and offers to save the orphan girl from that inferno, taking her by canoe through the jungle to the remotest part of the forest, where the Old Wizard reigns, sworn enemy of the giant grasshoppers. (Depending on how late it was, a variety of animals ranging from real to mythological might make their appearance during this part of the story.) The Old Wizard welcomes the orphan girl with affection and generosity. For seven years he feeds, clothes, and instructs her. The magic doll, however, is progressively dominated by terrible jealousy, which leads her to demand the orphan girl's banishment. The orphan by then has become very beautiful, and she seduces animals and plants of the forest, reducing the powers of the Old Wizard by half. Weakened by love, the Old Wizard is reluctant to banish the orphan girl from his domain. Strengthened by hate, the magic doll insists. They argue. They fight. The orphan girl overhears one of these disputes and realizes that her only hope is to unite herself with the Old Wizard against the magic doll. But meanwhile, she makes a fearful discovery: she has fallen in love with the doll. (Here, sometimes, there were long digressions into the mutual games of seduction between the orphan and the doll.) Corralled, but not losing her good sense, the orphan girl then transfers her allegiance to the magic doll and confesses her love. (We never understood this part too well.) The doll glows from this revelation. Together, the two of them lure the weakened Old Wizard into a dungeon. After the bars are closed upon him, doll and orphan meld together into one being, which flies over the forests toward the horizon. The Old Wizard, who foresaw everything, grasps his bars with trembling hands and, eyes fixed on the sublime being that grows smaller and smaller in the moonlight, sings his tango."

But Silvana falls silent, head bowed, busy confirming her recollections. No matter how great my curiosity is, I won't commit the indiscretion of asking if, after all these years, she can still remember the lyrics or melody of that tango. Not even Guilhermina herself had been capable of quoting precisely to Andrea the aria the Honorable had sung with his last breath. . . . No, what Silvana is looking for is something else.

"He had no shadow. Like any self-respecting wizard, the one in our story had no shadow. And he suffered greatly because of this. But during the tango, as he sang, he suddenly saw his shadow growing under his feet. His happiness was enormous. At this point in the story, Guilhermina always managed to project a huge shadow on the walls of our bedroom, and at the same time, with her back to us, she would flap her arms beside the window, flying toward the dark night sky."

She spreads her arms out diagonally and stretches up in her chair, as if she were about to fly into the arms of the waiter, who rushes away.

"Then, she would throw herself onto our bed and split her sides laughing at us!"

Silvana looks straight at me and chuckles. But quickly she recomposes herself and changes her manner.

"She was good at telling stories, Guilhermina was. And she was beautiful. She was beautiful when she spun her tales, when she sewed our costumes, and when she stood in her canoe, red hair blowing in the wind and her lacy white bridal dress caught up around her knees . . . that's how I always remember her, flying in her stories, or gliding across the water in front of us."

Chapter Twenty-six

The man in jeans and a white shirt with rolled-up sleeves must be around forty. He works swiftly and with determination. From the top of his ladder, almost touching the high ceiling, he yells down to me:

"Make yourself at home, I'll be right with you."

My steps echo on the floor of the empty living room. The smell of paint takes me to the open window. I now understand better his hesitation on the phone when I insisted he see me today: he's just starting the paint job on his small apartment in Rue Campagne Première, and there's a lot of work ahead of him. But the beautiful view from the sixth floor renders homage to the clear spring skies. And his good-humored voice behind me reflects the same cheerfulness.

"I'm sorry I can't even offer you some coffee. . . ."

His gesture sweeps across the empty room and includes the furniture covered with white sheets visible in the bedroom to one side. Henri Nat rubs his hands vigorously on a cleaning rag before shaking mine. He pulls a rather smashed pack of cigarettes from his hip pocket, offers me a Gitane, comes over to the window, and, looking out over the roofs of Montparnasse, goes directly to the point.

"You said on the phone you wanted to ask me some questions about my father. May I know for what reason?"

"Of course."

I apologize once again for insisting on meeting him today. I explain that I had a hard time finding him and that I am going back to my country at the beginning of next week.

"It doesn't matter at all. I'm the one who should apologize, receiving you here in such a mess."

The sentences, articulate and precise in his mouth, come out unpolished and hesitant from mine. But we are both sincere, which is all that matters. The little pause that follows, nevertheless, is more significant than words: either I produce a convincing answer, or I will be faced with one more *je regrette*. I discard my well-rehearsed little speech and take a calculated risk:

"Did the wallpaper in this room once have scenes on it from Watteau?"

"Watteau? No. Why?"

But the question has obviously intrigued him. He looks at me with interest and adds, almost at once,

"Though actually, a long time ago . . ."

He stops, taking a drag on his cigarette. He folds his arms, saying what crosses his mind:

"You're not old enough to have been here then."

My back to the window, I point to the wall in front of me.

"The piano used to be here, right? Opposite the window, facing that wall?"

He smiles and nods. "Right, the old piano was always there, ever since I was a child. You can still see the marks on the floor. And I do remember the Watteau scenes on the walls, although the name, at that time, meant nothing to me. I was always impressed by the somber colors. . . . But may I ask . . ."

He pauses and his eyes, newly alight with interest, complete the question. I've got his attention, but it would be a mistake to continue with my little guessing games. I hold up my hands.

"I apologize. I certainly don't want to give you the wrong impression."

I recite my little story. I've repeated it so often I actually begin to believe it. At bottom, it's true: am I or am I not involved in a sort of research project? The answer I give myself serves to inject some sincerity into the words I enunciate; when I finish, Henri Nat seems reassured.

"Interesting work, yours. Very interesting."

But his face reveals nothing about what he knows, or what he thinks. Still, he appears to be making a decision. He gives me a small look, as if he were about to turn down a road with no return. Another drag on the cigarette, and he gestures me to come into the bedroom. *The small vase of poppies between the books on the shelf, your red hair against the white sheets like a Renoir . . .* The sheet he raises reveals a nightstand, probably a twin of the one that had circulated through Guilhermina's life. Kneeling, Henri opens the bottom drawer, and takes from it a little sheaf of papers. They are musical scores: Poulenc, Satie, Fauré, Ravel. Despite the speed with which Henri leafs through them, I notice that some of the scores have dedications. Finally he finds the one he's looking for.

"My father wrote this. He dedicated it to her. A trio for piano, violin, and cello. He never wanted to have it published. As far as I know, the piece wasn't ever played outside this room."

He jerks a thumb over his shoulder to indicate the living room behind us. I open the score. It is entitled *Goddess of the Sea Spray*. I can't resist the temptation:

"It's a reference to a verse of Théodore de Banville."

"Really? How do you know?"

"An inscription found on the back of an old photograph taken in Nice."

"A photo of my father? With her? From before the war then . . . could I see it?"

"That's possible. Maybe I can send you a copy. But probably your father kept a copy too."

181

He shakes his head doubtfully.

"I would have seen it, especially after he died. I'm his only heir, I lost my mother when I was a child. No, actually there weren't many photos of his youth. I have almost nothing from the period before he married my mother."

His eyes go back to the musical score in my hands.

"I don't even know if the trio is any good. My father wasn't a great musician."

His tone is calm, as if not being a great musician were a comparatively unimportant detail in the career of a pianist and composer. From my expression he realizes his remark sounds odd, and tries to frame his thought more clearly.

"He was friends with all the well-known musicians of his day, and circulated among their group. He wasn't a bad pianist; he gave recitals here and abroad as well. He was an excellent teacher. But as a composer, I would say he didn't get too far."

Back to the score again.

"In fact, if I recall correctly, it's possible that not even she . . . what was her name again?"

"Guilhermina."

"Right, Guilhermina . . . It's possible that not even she ever heard this trio played."

The information falls strangely on our ears, as if Guilhermina's possible lack of interest might now cause some awkwardness between us. Almost at once, as if trying to make up for any indelicacy, he adds:

"In any case, from what he told me, he composed this work after she went back to Brazil."

He continues, still worried,

"You're welcome to take a copy of it, if you're interested. By the way, have you had lunch?"

"Not yet."

"Good. Down below there's a shop where you can make photocopies, and on the corner there's a little restaurant where, if you like, we could eat together and talk more at our ease. It'll give the first coat of paint time to dry. The *patron* is an old friend of mine and the restaurant's an oasis in Montparnasse, changed as it is today. It's a somewhat anachronistic place. I have lunch there almost every Sunday. *D'accord?"*

"D'accord."

"On weekends they make excellent tripe."

To his way of thinking, this is a definitive argument, one which puts everything back in its proper place, as if the prospect of eating something, particularly a special dish, should be in itself able to re-establish the harmony between past and present. A possible awkwardness brought about by the involuntary ingratitude of a woman toward a minor composer could never prevail over tripe moistened by good wine. We close the door behind us and descend the six floors, talking animatedly about Brazil, my work at the university, and the weeks I've spent in Paris.

"My father sent me some postcards from your country. You know, he stopped there, in 1952 or '53, on his way back from Buenos Aires."

"I know."

"I was four years old. I have those postcards to this day, in some briefcase or other. He brought me some huge maracas as a souvenir, from Rio. Did you know he had been to Brazil?"

"Yes."

"Through her?"

"Yes, indirectly."

Our arrival at the shop interrupts our conversation. While the copies are being made, I examine my surroundings. Almost talking to myself, I inquire,

"Wasn't there once a small art gallery where this shop is now?"

The clerk, a Portuguese woman, doesn't know. I go outside onto the sidewalk. As I look up, I see again the apartment we have just left, with its half-open windows. I bend toward the shop front,

---

183

looking for the Mirós that had fascinated Guilhermina in another era. Henri comes up to me.

"You're right. The proprietor just confirmed it: there was a small art gallery here once. But that was—"

"I know, before the war."

"Exactly. How did you know?"

"Your father met her again on this very sidewalk."

The copies are ready. As I pay for them Henri stands outside, looking at the sidewalk under his feet, as if he were seeing it for the first time and glimpsing his very young father promenading arm in arm with a woman whose profile was one of fire and dreams. All four of us walk toward the restaurant. Arm in arm, so to speak. Indeed, today they are cooking tripe. My companion is very well known here. The *patron* comes out from behind the counter to greet him. I am introduced as a friend from Brazil. *"Ah, le Brésil,"* they exclaim among themselves, as if that were enough. A faint perfume of exotic tropical jungles is mingled for a few seconds with the aromas that waft from the kitchen and pleasantly greet our nostrils. The restaurant is still empty. The *patron* brings three glasses and a bottle and sits down with us, serving us each a couple of fingers of red wine. We drink to the health of Brazil and France. The *patronne* also raises her glass from behind the counter. Then she yells,

"Etienne!"

An old, sleepy-looking waiter comes out of the room at the back and, dragging his feet a little, presents the menu, which Henri passes directly to me. He already knows what he wants. I let Guilhermina choose. To my horror she confirms: *tripes à la mode de Caen*. But first she orders oysters.

"Elles sont très bonnes," the owner assures me.

Just as I'm closing the menu, a dish indicated as the accompaniment for another item catches my eye: *Tomates Clamart!* On

pure impulse, I ask if I may have these tomatoes with my tripe. My companions exchange a look. The owner says, *"Tout est possible pour le Brésil."* I've definitely committed a serious gastronomical gaffe. Never mind. Each of us manages the ironies of fate as best he can.

Chapter Twenty-seven

My father used to talk to me for hours on end when I was a child. I had lost my mother very early, and we kept each other company. He would talk constantly about the artists he had known in his youth. Paris in the twenties and thirties was another city. And this neighborhood, which was his, and today is so disfigured as to be almost unrecognizable, lived its days of glory—poetry, bohemia, nonchalance."

"*C'était la belle époque, quoi,*" the *patron* confirms, confusing his eras a little and swallowing two generations and a war in the process.

The oysters have come and gone, the tripe is on its way, and the *patron* continues to sit at our table, controlling with one eye the comings and goings about the room, and with the other, the door through which more customers enter. Many wave to him or come over and greet us. Some have the right to their own napkins, in rings, which Etienne takes from the drawer of a buffet near the kitchen door.

I praise the familiar atmosphere of the little restaurant. I tell the *patron* that a few years back, I earned a living as a cook in an Italo-Brazilian restaurant in Los Angeles. He asks me a few questions about this phase of my life, and laughs broadly at my adventures in Cyrano's kitchen. He explains that a restaurant, in France, is never just a business. For those who cook, those who serve the tables, and those who come to eat, a restaurant is like an extension of their own—

Henri finishes for him. "—their own family. And the family is the basis for everything!"

We stop, awaiting more details. Henri seems to realize that his remark requires further elaboration, particularly on an almost-empty stomach. But he doesn't seem anxious to supply it. Changing direction, he points a finger toward me.

"*Vous, par exemple.*"

His voice is rather loud. Henri is getting a little drunk. After all, it's Sunday. The two fingers of wine offered by the *patron* have given way to two carafes of Muscadet, and now a third follows, this time red house wine. ("Quite trustworthy," the *patron* assures me with a little wink.) Henri leans over the table toward me. The *vous* with which he distinguishes me is lost among the vapors of alcohol and cigarette smoke. We're already close friends.

"You. You probably had a father and mother during your childhood and adolescence, didn't you?"

"Yes."

"*Voilà. C'est ça la famille.*"

He leans back in his chair again. We all nod in agreement, Henri included. I start to ask myself if it was a good idea to accept his invitation to lunch. But I'm not really worried: first impressions hardly ever are the ones that count. Henri proceeds:

"You see, in my case, my mother's death brought me closer to my father, but in a curious fashion. For example, I could tell you several stories about my father's women—but none of them would have anything to do with my mother. Her death made us close, but close the way two adults are. And men rarely talk seriously about their deepest feelings. They may talk seriously about business. Or discuss in detail the next atom bomb. They may immediately afterward spend fortunes to deactivate it. They may debate the best

---

187

starters for a soccer team. But when it comes to the emotions . . ."

The shrug, his two hands upraised, seems sincere.

"And my father, in spite of being an artist, a lover of life, and sort of a backyard poet, was basically a man just like any other. That's why he never really talked to me about my mother."

The *patron* continues to nod his head, signifying unrestricted understanding and solidarity. He must have heard this same story countless times, with variations accompanying the changes in his menu. Tripe, melancholy; steak tartare, despair; trout in herb sauce, slightly indifferent levity. His sign to Etienne means: bring another bottle. Etienne yells from the other corner of the room:

"*Du rouge?*"

"*Du rouge!*"

And so it goes. The soul of the wines sings in the bottles, which seem to be floating in space around us. I imagine that the first coat of paint must have dried and redried by this time in the sixth-floor mansard apartment. Henri must be thinking: to hell with the apartment painting. I think: to hell with my last-minute shopping. With the help of the wine and the *patron*'s friendliness, of the spring light that filters through the windows, of the longing I suddenly feel for Andrea, and of Henri's revolt over his mother's death—with all these things and the rest that is still to come, we'll press on, we'll get beyond the three layers of paint that still separate us from Guilhermina and Watteau.

Henri asks,

"Do you understand?"

"I do. It's like *Five Easy Pieces*."

"What?"

"An American film. In the final sequence, Jack Nicholson pushes his father in a wheelchair through an open field. And it's then, with no time to lose, that he finally manages to tell his father he loves him. And the old father, who can no longer speak because he's totally paralyzed, weeps. Or so I remember. . . . Two tears run down his face."

"What would the title be in French?"

"I don't know. *Cinq pièces faciles?* But there must be forty French films that deal with the same theme, in one way or another."

"Forty? You're kidding . . . we 'invented' that theme!"

After a pause he continues, focused again on his past.

"Yes. In any case, I ended up learning a great deal, but always by sifting through things, a little here, a little there. I knew tons of things that children generally have no access to. Most were trivial episodes, but concerning men who were anything but trivial. Like the night Ravel tore up the first version of his *Bolero,* or Nijinsky running off with a *cascadeur,* or the terrible political hangover of Aragon when he returned from his historic trip to the Soviet Union. The differences of opinion between Erté and Lalique, the sequences that didn't work out in Marcel Carné's films. Some were true stories gathered from friends who worked with those people, others half invented, when the circumstances of the moment demanded it. Stories of Montparnasse—of artists and entrepreneurs, of bills never charged, of generous people victimized by petty beings. And stories of women—my father's and those of his friends. Sometimes, stories of the men those women had known. Stories that years later I encountered in the works of Henry Miller. Have you read Henry Miller?"

"Yes."

"He was a friend of my father's, my father is quoted in two of his stories. I'm called Henri because of him."

He gives me an accomplice's wink. He seems satisfied at being the trustee of so many stories. The *patron* is even more satisfied, as if through gastronomic affinities he too had access to this rich heritage. We're all satisfied. In a minute we'll be giving each other congratulatory pats on the back. But Henri suddenly stretches his arm across the table and pokes a finger lightly into my belly.

"Mais—surprise!—de la brésilienne, rien. Nothing, absolutely

189

nothing, about the Brazilian woman. An even greater silence than that enveloping my mother."

He stops to watch my reaction. Okay by me: finally someone who knows *nothing* about Guilhermina, a rarity in this city. It's better that way. Henri repeats sadly:

"Nothing about the Brazilian woman. Not a word about her. That in itself was alarming. To know so many useless things about people who probably didn't even count . . . and about her, only mystery and curiosity. Yet my father thought about her all the time; I could feel him thinking about her, like you think about a piece missing from your life, a piece that, if recovered, would perhaps give greater meaning to the whole. At first, when I was smaller, I thought that his melancholy moments were due to the loss of my mother. Later, very gradually, I started to realize that it wasn't my mother he was thinking about, when he would sit alone at the piano at night, playing a few disconnected notes. How I could tell it was the Brazilian woman, I don't know—intuition, I guess. I think it's even possible he might have dreamed of forming a family with her, at some time in his past. For him, family was—"

"Everything!" the *patron* quickly cuts in, waving to Etienne, who comes over to our table.

The *Tomates Clamart* are presented before us. I look at them fondly, with a certain sense of expectation, as if from the bottom of their dish they could wish me good afternoon, tell me of their origins, confirm to me the degree to which I can trust the present conversation, or reveal some secret about their ancestors. Henri proceeds, caught up in his memories.

"On one of the two postcards he sent from Rio to his sister— my aunt used to take care of me when he traveled—my father scribbled three sentences in pencil: *I saw her. She is married to a gentleman who wears a carnation in his lapel. She seems happy, so I tried to pretend that I was happy too.*"

His inner eye focuses once more on the gentleman with the carnation in his lapel. I sense that to him this gentleman is almost a

familiar personage, like an old uncle who remained unknown because he lived overseas. Three lines on a postcard; three coats of paint covering the Watteau wallpaper. I ask myself if one day I should send Henri the letters his father wrote to Guilhermina. *Why didn't you come yesterday? Was the food last Sunday really that bad? Guilhermina, what kind of surrender was that, followed so soon by a disappearance?*

Chapter Twenty-eight

Years later, when I was somewhat bigger, I found that postcard among some of my aunt's books, and I asked my father what those three sentences meant. He looked at me distantly, patted my head, and rather reluctantly opened the drawer where he kept his musical scores. In that small nightstand I just showed you. Then, with the trio in his hands, he told me a little about her. Not much; really almost nothing. He played some notes on his piano, absently, with his left hand, and I realized that they were the notes of the trio, the same notes and the same disconnected chords I had grown accustomed to hearing on his solitary nights, when I would play with my toy cars on the rug near the piano. Those notes confirmed my intuition that he was thinking of the Brazilian woman, not my mother, on those occasions. An intuition born from his music."

He stops, as if suspended between the chords. His tone changes.

"Of course, it's equally possible that I'm wrong, that he liked to improvise around those same notes for other reasons, or with other women in mind. I never dared to ask what that title meant, *Goddess of the Sea Spray*. It would have been too intimate a question between men, even though one was the other's little boy. Who would have guessed. Théodore de Banville . . .''

He looks at me without disguising a sincere admiration, as if I had cleared up some crucial enigma that would now permit us to open new horizons for the well-being of humanity. He rubs his eyes and dives back into the depths of his memory.

"Yes, and before he closed the drawer, I recall now, he said that the violin and the piano were like a couple sewing the melody together, trying to constitute a family, but the cello was the boss of the trio, distancing or bringing together the other two, like dark-colored plankton floating among fish in clear water. I remember that image very well, *dark-colored plankton floating in clear water*. And he never brought up the subject again. He didn't really need to, did he?"

The tripe makes its triumphal entry. It's a good thing, as I'm nearly falling to the floor, overwhelmed by the wine, the cellos and violins that multiply around us in a whirlwind of planktons orchestrated by nightstands.

"C'est quand même beau le cello!" exclaims the *patron,* to salute the food and drive away for good the melancholy that was creeping up on our table.

We toast the piano, the cello, and the violin. We toast the tripe, I praying inwardly that it has been very, very well cleaned. We drink to the prosperity of our respective countries and the well-being of our peoples. One more toast and I will make a speech. The *patron* orders more wine. Together with the new bottle, Etienne brings more plates and silverware. The *patronne,* glass in hand, sits at the table with us; the four of us will eat together. *"Bon appétit, Monsieur. Merci Madame."* Henri, more lively than ever, goes on, fork in the air:

"One afternoon, just a few months before he died, he showed me the sheet music of his friends. He told me that one day they would probably be worth something. And it's true, almost all the scores were signed by people who are famous today. He was very much loved by his friends. But when he saw the trio he had com-

193

posed for his Brazilian, he only said, 'Nobody will want this one. *Mais garde-la tout de même,* who knows, one day . . .' "

Here he has a sudden idea:

"Maybe I should give you the original? And keep the copy?"

"But why?"

"I don't know . . . because today is a special day, today's Sunday, on Sunday some things finish, and others begin. . . ."

"Vive le dimanche! Etienne, l'addition de la quatre!" ("Here's to Sunday! Etienne, the check for table four!")

"And also because something might have crossed his mind when he asked me to keep that score. Maybe a hunch about our meeting . . ."

"Thanks, but I don't know if I should accept."

"Why not?"

"Because it doesn't seem like . . ."

"Maybe you can give me something in exchange . . ."

"Such as?"

"I don't know . . . her story . . . Why don't you tell us her story?"

"Her story . . . it's very long, and full of large blank spaces. I only know a few parts of it."

"But it's a long Sunday, too, full of large blank spaces. . . . *Etienne, l'addition de la deux! Au revoir, Raphael! À demain!"* ("Etienne, the check for table two. 'Bye, Rafael. See you tomorrow!")

"Quelle histoire?" asks the *patronne,* who must be a little deaf.

"Monsieur a connu une amie du père d'Henri. . . ." ("The gentleman knew a friend of Henri's father.")

"Ah. Tell us something about her . . . what was her name?"

"Guilhermina."

"Guilhermina. Did she do something extraordinary?"

"She killed a man."

"Qu'est-ce qu'il dit?" ("What is he saying?")

"Qu'elle a tué un homme." ("That she killed a man.")

"Ah . . . a long time ago?"

"Yes."

"Did she really kill a man? Honestly? And that's the end of the story? But my dear fellow, you start at the end? That's not worth an original musical score. . . . I take back my offer. If Schubert had started at the end, we would never have had the Unfinished Symphony!"

He doubles up with laughter at his own joke. In spite of so much wine, I'm having difficulty laughing along with him.

"That was in the beginning, or almost. Well, things happened before and things happened after. Before, she crossed a river with her bridal dress pulled up to her knees; after, she rode an elephant in Istanbul; before, she patiently built up a modest collection of dolls; after, she took care of four green dwarfs; before, she was madly in love with her older brother; after, she gave herself to a man in a balloon and a woman on a train. More or less like the befores and afters of your cyclical wars."

I stop, worried that I may be emitting too many signals at the same time and boring my companions. But in fact, and fortunately for them, they all have their noses in their food and are busy evaluating its quality.

"Moreover, like the stories your father told you about himself and his friends, they might have been half-truths, small inventions, half-lies, it's hard to know. Sometimes people lie or omit things to embellish or to protect . . . or they add things, convinced that some fictitious event really did happen. Guilhermina may have lived much more than we know. For example, we know nothing about the man with the carnation in his lapel, at whose side she finally settled down for at least thirteen years, and whom your father met in Rio. Or, she may have lived to a much lesser degree than we think, just passing through life, sometimes greedily, sometimes very discreetly, in general indifferent to the realities of her time. My

---

generation would yell in chorus, perhaps rightly: 'Alienated!' But we don't even know that for certain, because nothing is left of her last thirty years, except a vague reference to an orphanage."

I take advantage of the general silence around me to get reacquainted with my wineglass. Then I continue:

"There were times when I was very close to her, as if she were flesh and blood and I could actually touch her. Other times, she seemed more like a comic-strip figure who had locked up her secrets in the drawer of an old desk and thrown the key into the ocean. On certain days I felt I was growing closer to her through the books she had read, on others I imagined she must have read some of them backward. Once, toward the end of her life, she said to a niece: 'I've been the same person ever since I was fourteen. But what person, I never knew.' How can we ever know what really happens in someone else's life?"

Everyone eats in silence. I talked a lot more than I should have; never mind. I promise myself not to open my mouth again until the coffee comes.

"You're right, you never know," comments the *patronne* after a long moment, shaking her head with the pensive smile of one who, at bottom, may not have understood very well what she heard, but manages to arrive at certain truths through having stewed some good secrets in her pots and pans in the course of a well-lived life.

Henri observes me thoughtfully. His father must have lived a lot of stories . . . Something in his eyes reflects his father's experience, of which Henri became keeper, guardian, and sole heir. He raises his glass silently in my honor, and I toast him with the same discretion. Of the four of us, only the *patron* seems a person without mysteries. He smacks his lips in contentment and twirls his mustaches. Things have gone well this Sunday; the restaurant is full and his friend Henri is not depressed or drunk, as usually happens. Who knows, tomorrow he may be able to slip away and meet Claudine in her little room. He smiles affectionately at the *patronne*.

———

The last rays of spring sunshine produce a band of light that angles through the window and bathes our table in gold. My new friends nod sleepily, wrapped in old, unreachable memories. Guilhermina is on the scene, but she's not alone, she has company. Other characters from her past prop their elbows on the table among us. Suddenly, a fragment of reality breaks in, brought by the friendly voice of the *patronne*.

"How were the tomatoes?"

"Delicious. Really superb. My congratulations."

"A variation of the original recipe, a secret that's been in our family for generations."

"Really? How long?"

The *patron* interrupts, changing the course of the conversation and maybe of history:

"And you, what did you come to France to do?"

"I—"

"He came to get an old musical score."

A final effort on Henri's part to get me back on track. But my tomatoes are gone, this time forever. I recount my perambulations through Paris, the classes, the film projections, the reactions of the students and the general public. We talk about Brazil and France, their similarities and differences, the little details that countries and cities incessantly invent to postpone the great leap into the communal gulf. We talk of Rio de Janeiro. I mention that Rio was French long before it was Portuguese or even Brazilian. I speak of Villegaignon, one of the 16th century French colonizers, and of his adventures in Brazil. I remind my listeners that, in those days, our Indians loved to feast on invading French navigators—but hasten to add that this rampant cannibalism had been, in recent years, replaced by an appetite, almost as ferocious, for French fashion, ideas, bonbons, and perfume. I mention the Garnier and Briguiet bookstore, the Café Provenceaux (*meublé, tapissé, rideauné à la mode de Paris*), the three visits of Sarah Bernhardt to Rio de Janeiro, Anatole France's speech to the Brazilian Academy of Letters, the influence

197

of Le Corbusier on every street corner. My listeners seem as genuinely surprised with these stories as the green dwarfs had been with Guilhermina's giant grasshoppers. But when dessert comes, Henri, mouth taken up by a splendid strawberry, insists for the last time:

"None of that! No more rampant cannibalism! Our Brazilian friend really came to Paris to find an old musical score! A score dedicated to the Goddess of the Sea Spray!"

All eyes converge upon me. There's no way to escape. I stand up, raise my glass, and, trying to disguise my timidity, recite in my heroic French:

" 'Nice, like you, a goddess laughing and vibrant, emerging from a jet of foam beneath the kiss of the sun . . .' "

General applause, bravos, glasses raised in my honor. I feel as if I had finally paid back the historic visit of Anatole France to Rio. Even old Etienne, who is slowly clearing the tables, joins us. "To the Goddess!" I come back to earth and sit down again, acknowledging the applause. Next time, I promise myself, I'll do even better.

The afternoon breeze comes through the open windows. Etienne sweeps the dust and cigarette butts from the floor out onto the sidewalk. A dog puts its head over the threshold of the door, stares at our group, and runs off, wagging its tail. We drink our coffee in silence, the real world emerging little by little through the steam rising from our cups. The chairs squeak. It's time to go, time to say good-bye. Two more days and I'll be on the plane home. It's a shame. So much to see, to say, to imagine, to guess . . .

Guilhermina, gazing out her window on the old coffee plantation, also watched imaginary landscapes parading incessantly before her. The longer she kept her eyes closed, the further she went. At first, borrowing images from the travels of her old husband. Later, resorting to her books and to the legends she had patiently accumulated in her memory. Finally, relying solely on her own reserve of dreams and energy.

Thanks to this, she must have glimpsed the four friends who

are now saying good-bye on the sidewalk before returning to their half-painted walls, their unpacked suitcases, their century-old recipes. Beyond these four people, behind the fields, the canvases, and the waiting worlds, she may have seen a whole panel of characters, of different ages, time periods, and sizes, who also embraced, souls cleansed and legs unsteady, mellowed by the wine and the sound of a musical piece finally resurrected. And before guiding her old husband down the steps toward the infinite, before trying a little of everything in the great world—always with the guilty haste of one who has stolen time from another person's life—she might perhaps have seen the flock of birds winging swiftly over the tree-tops to rise like arrows toward the heavens and surround a bright-colored balloon that floats between the clouds. From the balloon, small but visible in the late-afternoon light, a man waves his red-and-white cap to the people making their farewells on the sidewalk below. It is a small homage the landscape offers Guilhermina, who observes everything from her window. As if the landscape could wish her good luck.